Sunset Love

The first novel in
The Sunset Love Series

Missy Lynn
Copyright June 2011

Chapter 1

Finally, the last box in our new beachfront home was unpacked and I could relax a little. As I plopped down on the couch in walks my best friend and go-to-gal, Stephanie. Steph and I have known each other for so long she is more of a sister than a friend. We met when my husband, Jonathan, and her boyfriend, Steve, whom she had left to come to California with me, started working together offshore. When the guys would go offshore she and I would practically live together. She was there for the birth of all three of my children and like a second mother to them.

"Everything is finally done?" she asked

"Yeah," I sighed "Finally"

She sat down next to me. "So, what's our next step?" She could tell by the look on my face I was clueless.

We were from a small town near New Orleans called Houma, La and this was all new to us. Tragically a year before, Jonathan was killed in a horrible offshore accident. We had finally settled the lawsuit against the company he worked for and for the first time I felt peace.

"Well, Stephanie, I think our only choice right now is to get to know the area. We are living in the city of dreams so surely someone will help us. Let's get the kids ready for bed and turn in for the night."

As I lay in bed that night I remember some of the conversations Jonathan and I had. His dream for his children was that they would never do without and live their lives to the fullest. No matter what we had to do to make that possible. He was great with a guitar and had an amazing voice. He had always wanted to have a career in the music industry, but his parents were realists and pushed him away from his dream. After all that had happened I knew what I had to do. Life is too short to be unhappy. The kids shared their daddy's dream of being famous, so here we were in California.

Constance was only eight when Jonathan died. She shared her daddy's dream of being a famous singer. At her age, she has the talent and the looks. Her voice alone would make you melt, but when you add the big pretty blue eyes and curly blonde bouncing hair, she was the full package with an attitude to match. I don't see anyone pushing her around in this town.

Charlie was only seven and didn't seem to care about anything. Every day he was more and more the spitting image of his daddy with his short brown curls and his sparkling grey eyes surrounded by eyelashes that would make any girl jealous. He had the look and probably the talent, but nobody knew because he stayed to himself all the time and never let it show.

Drew was only five, but he was a daddy's boy and also wanted to make his daddy proud by becoming famous. He hasn't quite come into the talent part yet, but he definitely has the look. I could just be a proud mama but he is always being told his dimples will steal the show. Mix that with his longish blonde straight hair, his piercing blue eyes and the chubby cheeks he hasn't grown out of yet and he is definitely made for television.

I must have dozed off because the next thing I knew I had three very excited kids jumping on my bed hollering in unison. "Mama lets go to the beach! Come on mom, get up! We want to go to the beach today!"

Drew stopped jumping on the bed, sat down next to me, and looked up at me with those puppy dog eyes. "Mom, may we please go to the beach today?"

We were unpacked and settled in so why not enjoy a day of lounging by the ocean. "Sure we can. Go get Stephanie up and we will go." With that off the kids went.

We stepped out our back door and onto the beach. It looked like paradise. Stephanie and I set up the chairs while the kids were playing at the edge of the water. Constance and Drew were singing and reenacting songs and scenes from one of their all-time favorite movies "The Day the Stars Fell" starring Michael Stargate while Charlie was sitting by himself digging in the sand.

"It looks like the kids are settling in good," Stephanie said.

"Yeah I just hope I don't have my hands full," I said. We both started laughing.

"You know that is going to happen." she said. Our laughter was stopped by a shrill scream I knew came from Constance. I looked up and she and Drew were running down the beach as fast as their legs would carry them.

"Y'all get back over here or we are going inside," I yelled. Constance stopped, turned around with Drew in tow. Before she got back to where we were I could see she was crying.

She shouted through the tears streaming down her face, "Mom why did you stop us? That was Michael! I saw Michael!

"Michael who, Constance? I don't care who it was, you don't go running off like that." I said as I dried her tears.

"But mom that was Michael Stargate. I just wanted to meet him. He is one of my favorite actors."

I realized then whom she thought she had seen. "Constance, I'm sure that wasn't him. There are many people that look like him around here. Just do not go running off again. Famous or not you don't talk to strangers do you understand?"

"Yes ma'am." She replied as she stomped off.

As I watched the sun set over the ocean I felt we

had a successful first day. Though the day was uneventful, nobody got hurt physically and everybody had a good time. Constance was playing her guitar on the back deck while Drew sang along and, of course, Charlie was in his room reading. I was deep in thought when I heard that shrill scream again that I knew only belonged to Constance. As I made it to the back door I could hear talking and it was a voice I knew all too well. It was Michael Stargate.

"Hi there. I hear you playing and your friend singing and wanted to come meet you," He said.

"I'm not her friend, I'm her brother silly," Drew said laughing.

Constance cut him a dirty look and whispered, "Drew we aren't supposed to talk to him."

She turned back to Michael and politely said, "My mama said I couldn't talk to strangers, even if you are famous."

Michael laughed shyly. "So you know I'm famous, huh?"

Constance jumped up. "Yeah I love your movie 'The Day the Stars Fell'! I mean I'm sorry but I can't talk to strangers. I'm really, really sorry."

"It's okay," Michael said, "Maybe if I meet your mommy then you can talk to me because we wouldn't be strangers anymore."

As I walked outside Drew jumped up. "Mama, Constance was talking to this famous stranger!" She cut him another dirty look, mumbling under her breath "tattletale," and quickly turned to me.

"Mom I tried really hard not to talk to him, but he is just so cute. I did try really hard,"

Michael started laughing and stretched his hand out, "Hi, I'm Michael-"

I interrupted chuckling "Oh trust me, I know exactly who you are. The kids watch your movie at least

5

once a week. I'm Sherri. It's nice to meet you."

Michael Stargate was a sight with his sparkling blue eyes and shaggy sandy blonde hair blowing in the breeze coming off the beach.

Constance started jumping up and down. "Awesome mom! Now he isn't a stranger. Can I talk to him now? Can I, can I, can I?"

Before I could give her an answer her attention was on Michael. "You are so good on TV. I want to be like that someday." She was blushing.

"Well I heard you playing from the beach. Can you sing too?"

"Well I can sing, but Drew usually does the singing."

"Yeah, I heard him singing," as he patted Drew on the head. "You're not too bad but you will grow into it I'm sure. How old are you?"

"I'm five," he said as he came running to hide behind me.

Constance started to play and sing. Michael's eyes were fixed on her as he walked over to me. "She has an amazing voice. Has she had voice lessons?"

I started blushing now. "No it's all her. Her daddy started teaching her to play the guitar when she was just two and it has just gone from there. Since her daddy was killed she seems to throw herself into music. I guess that's not a bad thing though."

His posture changed and he was no longer focused on Constance. "I'm so sorry to hear about your husband. Do you mind if I ask what happened?"

I opened my mouth to speak but was interrupted. "Mom when are we eating? I'm hungry," announced Drew while tugging on my shorts.

"I'm sorry. It was nice to meet you, but I need to get dinner started." I reached out to shake his hand, but before I

6

could Constance was between us.

"But mom! What if Michael stays for dinner? Please mom, please, please, please." She was begging.

As I looked into her eyes, "Now Constance, Michael is a big star. He probably has other things to do than to have dinner with a bunch of strangers."

Constance, who has an answer for everything, "But mom we aren't strangers anymore. We know each other now."

Michael started laughing. "I'm thinking she really wants me to stay for dinner."

"Well you're welcome to but I'm not so sure you would like what we eat," I said laughing. "We don't eat fancy around here."

He chuckled. "I'm sure whatever you fix will be fine."

Before anyone could say anything else Constance and Drew were running in the house yelling, "Michael is staying for dinner!! Michael is staying for dinner!!"

Michael opened the door for me like a gentleman. As I walked in he asked, "So what's for dinner?"

I was blushing and didn't realize it, "I guess whatever I can find in the kitchen."

He looked at me amazed. "You do your own cooking? I know where you can get a good maid. I know you're new in the area. I don't mind helping any way I can."

My thoughts were all over the place. I was insulted that he thought I needed a maid first of all, but on the other hand I had a cute superstar offering to help in any way. "No thanks. I like to do it myself. If I don't do it then it won't be done right. But thanks for the offer," I said laughing. *Great! Now he probably thinks I'm crazy.*

In the kitchen Michael was sitting at the bar talking to me while I was cooking. Stephanie came in not seeing him sitting there. "Constance said we were having royalty for dinner," she said laughing.

Michael stood up. "Well I wouldn't necessarily say royalty," he said smiling. He reached out to shake her hand. She was so stunned she couldn't move. I heard her say "Oh my God," as she ran out of the kitchen.

"I'm sorry about that," I laughed. "She isn't very good under pressure."

Michael sat back down "Its okay. I'm used to it. Happens all the time."

Constance and Drew come running in the kitchen dragging Charlie along. "See, I told you we had a superstar in our house. He is staying for dinner too," Constance danced around saying.

Charlie being Charlie walked over and politely extended his hand to shake Michaels. "Nice to meet you," he said, unimpressed. "Can I go now, mom?"

"Well Charlie wouldn't you like to talk to Mr. Michael?"

He looked at Michael, "No offense Mr. Michael, but I was busy."

Michael bent down and put his hand on Charlie's shoulder "Its okay man. I understand. Not everybody cares about what we care about do they?" Charlie smiled at him. It was the first time I had seen a real smile since Jonathan had died.

"It was nice to meet you, Mr. Michael, but I have things to do. I guess I will see you at dinner." He turned and ran back to his room.

I found myself smiling at Michael. "That's the first time since his daddy died that I have seen an actual smile out of him. Thank you for that."

"It's not hard. I like kids," he said.

I started laughing. "I guess it's not hard since you're still a kid yourself."

He looked at me bewildered. "I am not. I'm sure there isn't much age difference between us. I just look really young."

I was still laughing. "Yeah, you have to be what, sixteen, maybe seventeen?"

He was disgusted at that remark. "I will have you know I'm twenty-four, thank you very much. And just how old are you?"

My mouth was on the floor. "I'm so sorry. I really thought you were much younger than that."

He had such a baby face it was hard to believe he was as old as he was claiming.

He laughed. "Yeah well I look that young which is why I can play all the younger parts. Works out great for me because my career should be great before I get old. But you didn't answer my question."

Old? What did he consider old? I guess the definition of old in this city was much different than where we came from.

I looked at him trying to come up with a way around this. "What was the question?"

He laughed. "How old are you? You don't look like you can be much older than me if at all."

Constance saved me. "Mama, Mama, Mama! Can we get out the karaoke machine? Please, Please, Please!"

"No, Constance. Dinner is about done. Why don't you and Drew set the table for me?" She stomped to the counter where the plates were and off they went to set the table.

Michael got up. "I'm going to go help them."

I had avoided answering his question. He was right. I wasn't much older than him, but I didn't want to tell him how old I was either. I was only three years older than him, but felt much older and wasn't sure if that constituted old or not. My thoughts were interrupted. "Is there anything I

9

can do to help?" Michael had come back in the kitchen.

"No thank you. I think we are ready to eat."

As we sat down to eat, Stephanie came in trying not to look at Michael.

"So is she going to even look at me?" he asked quietly.

"Well I doubt it. She is really shy. Try talking to her and see what happens." She came and sat at the table with us barely looking at anyone.

"So are you scared to talk to me, Stephanie?"

She never looked at him. "No."

He looked at me, smiled and asked, "So, will you talk to me?"

Again never looking at him she said, "Sure."

We both started laughing. "Stephanie its okay to look at me. I'm not going to think you're crazy if you do." She smiled, looking up at him finally. "So how do you like California, Steph? Is it okay if I call you that?" You could see her tension starting to ease.

"Yes that's fine. It's okay-"

Before she could finish Drew interrupted. "We moved here 'cause my daddy blew up and is never coming back."

I reached over and put my hand on his shoulder. "Drew that's not nice to talk about at the dinner table. Let's talk about something else."

Michael looked at me taken aback and put his hand on my shoulder giving me an understanding glance. As I looked into his beautiful blue eyes I thought I was going to melt. I hadn't felt like this since I met Jonathan.

The moment was broken by Constance. "Mom, can we get the karaoke machine out after dinner? Please? Please?"

"I guess that would be ok. We need to check the acoustics in our new house anyway," I said smiling.

With part of my settlement money I bought a flat level house right on the beach. It was no mansion but for California it was fairly nice. There were twelve foot vaulted ceilings with a chandelier as you walk in the front door and a spiral staircase that led up to a small loft, which we used for the kids play room. The kitchen opened up into a step-down living room. On the other side of the house were the bedrooms. The house sat in a cul-de-sac with a back deck that ended just feet from the beach.

Constance immediately turned her attention to Michael. "Mr. Michael, do you want to sing with me?"

I interrupted her, "Whoa there missy. Mr. Michael is a busy man. He already stayed for dinner. He has a lot to do so let's not try to take up all his time."

Michael got up from the table, walked over and bent down, "I would LOVE to sing with you, if it's okay with your mom, that is. I don't want to wear out my welcome on your first day here," he said smiling at me.

"Mom, Mr. Michael didn't ask to be excused." Drew was yelling.

"Sorry Michael. My son, the courtesy police."

He laughed "Its okay Drew. I wasn't done with this awesome meal your mom cooked." As he sat down I was lost in thought again. He was polite, super cute, seemed to love kids, and made me want to melt. Sounded like a keeper to me.

"Mom!" Constance was yelling at me. "Are you ok? You're not listening to me!"

I snapped out of it. "Yes dear. What did you say?"

She looked at me irritated, "I said 'may I please be excused'?"

"I'm sorry, Constance. Yes you may."

Getting up, Michael helped me clean off the table. "So…" I knew what he was about to ask, "Your husband?"

It was a conversation I didn't really want to have

with someone I just met but I had gotten used to telling the story. "Jonathan and I were married for 9 years. He worked on offshore oil rigs. I was watching TV one day and saw there was a huge explosion." As I was telling the story I started shaking. Michael walked over, took the plates from me, put them on the counter and put his hand around my shoulders to help steady me.

"You don't have to tell me if it's too painful. I will understand. I'm sure this won't be the last time we see each other."

I looked at him still trying to regain my composure. "No its ok. I didn't realize it would affect me this way. I'm so sorry." He helped me over to the stool, sat me down and took my hand. "When I heard about the explosion I thought I was going to die until they said which rig it was. Jonathan wasn't working on that rig. I calmed down and kept up with the news on it. When I didn't hear from him that night I started to worry so I put in a call to his supervisor. It was three days before I knew that my husband actually had been working on that rig." I started to cry. Michael put his arm around me and started wiping the tears.

"You don't have to go on."

I looked up at him. "No I'm past the hard part." I dried my eyes and continued, "It turned out the company was not following the guidelines put out by the government. They were trying to save money and took away the love of my life and my children's father. I filed a lawsuit against them and once it was settled I decided the only way to spend the money was to make Jonathan's dreams for our kids come true. So here we are."

He looked at me like he was hanging on every word. When I finished he put his arms around me. As he held me, my thoughts weren't of Jonathan anymore. I could only think about my body feeling like Jell-O being in his arms. It was the first time I thought I might be able to start

12

my life over and really be happy with someone else.

Snap out of it Sherri! You just met this guy and you know nothing about him. You're just scared to do this on your own and it could never work anyway. He is a handsome, big star and you're a single mom from a small town. Life is not like the movies so wake up and stop dreaming.

We both jumped when Constance came running in. "The karaoke machine is set up. Let's go! Let's go! Let's go!" I looked at her. She stopped, composed herself, and said "Please."

Michael looked at me. "I think she is ready to sing."

I smiled at him. "This child is ALWAYS ready to sing."

In the living room Constance had everything set up and ready to go. "Mom, are you going to get the video camera?" I looked at Michael who appeared unconcerned. "Mom always videos us when we sing." She informed him.

Michael looked over at me and I looked like a deer caught in the headlights. "Well mom, are you going to get the camera?" Michael picked.

I laughed as I got up and got the camera. "I didn't want to do anything without your permission, Michael. I won't video you. I will just video the kids."

He looked at me bemused and asked, "And why wouldn't you?" Now I was the one confused. "You can take video of me, pictures of me, anything you want. If it's something you don't need or aren't supposed to have I will definitely let you know."

"I'm just not sure how things work around here yet. I wouldn't want to make an enemy out of our first new friend in California."

He just smiled at me. "I don't think we will have a problem with that at all."

It was around midnight and everybody was

exhausted. "Mom, one more thing before we go to bed?" This time it was Drew who was asking although I'm pretty sure Constance put him up to it.

"What's that sweetheart?"

He looked at Michael, smiled, and asked, "Would it be okay if this one time Mr. Michael put us to bed instead of you?"

I was stunned. They had not gone to bed without me since Jonathan died. "Let's give Mr. Michael a break why don't we? He has spent practically the whole night with us and I'm sure he is tired and ready to go home."

Michael picked up Drew tickling him. "I think your mom is tired of me being here and is being nice about it."

Drew looked at him and quipped, "No, my mom doesn't sugar coat things. If she didn't want you here she would tell you to leave."

Michael laughed. "Well okay then. Let's see about getting you kids to bed. Anything special I'm supposed to do mom?" he asked.

"No, just get them in bed and to go to sleep." I couldn't bear the thought of them going to bed without me but I knew this was something they really wanted so I snuck to their door and listened as he said goodnight to them.

"Will you be here in the morning?" Charlie asked.

"Well, I don't know Charlie. Do you want me to be?"

I almost fainted when I heard the answer. "Yes please." Charlie had been a recluse since his father died. He hadn't wanted to have anything to do with anyone or anything. Him wanting Michael there in the morning was monumental. I managed to get back in the living room on the couch without being detected eavesdropping.

"They are all tucked in and fast asleep." He said as he came in.

14

"I appreciate all the time you spent with them today. I know you're really busy and your girlfriend probably misses you by now. Since the kids are in bed you're welcome to make a graceful exit."

He walked over and sat next to me. "First of all, I don't have a girlfriend and secondly, if I didn't want to be here I would have left already. I was kind of hoping we could talk……unless you're ready for bed."

I looked at him crazy. "Look I understand you're a big superstar and have girls fall into bed with you but I'm not one of them."

He put his finger over my mouth. "That's not what I meant. I can see where you would take it that way, but not at all what I meant. I want to get to know you. I want to talk for a while, but if you're ready to go to bed I can see myself out." I was so embarrassed I know I turned eight shades of red. "If you don't mind me staying I can give you the info about the city, what to expect, what not to expect, and kind of help you out. Plus, I would love to know more about you. What brought you here, what your plans are while you're here, those kinds of things?"

"Sure you can stay if you would like. I was about to clean the kitchen but you're welcome to talk to me while I do that." I was flabbergasted that a big star like him was so interested in my family and me.

"How about I help you do that. Then it will get done faster." When he said that I thought I would wake up anytime now and realize it was all a dream.

While we cleaned the kitchen the conversation was light. We mostly talked about his career and his dreams. Stephanie had made herself scarce after dinner so it was just he and I. For the first time in a long time I felt comfortable with someone but I barely knew him, which threw me off guard. Once we got done with the kitchen I fixed us a drink and we went back in the living room.

"After Jonathan died I decided to move out here to help the kids. Constance and Drew both want to be singers and actors. Charlie….I don't know what he wants. Ever since Jonathan's death he barely comes out of his room."

Michael was looking in my eyes. "He asked me if I was going to be here in the morning."

I smiled. "Yeah he is probably hoping you're not. He doesn't like to be around people."

Michael smiled, "Well then I feel special. I asked him if he wanted me to be and he said yes."

I tried to look shocked, but I had heard it when he said it so it wasn't as surprising. "Well like I told you before, I'm not like that. I don't care how famous you are," I said smirking.

He leaned over and kissed me gently on the cheek. "And I told you that's not what I'm here for. Not all movie stars are like that. I have real feelings just like everybody else. All I want for you and your family is to be happy and enjoy living here. Your daughter has real talent and I think I can help you get her started on her career if you want."

I didn't know what to say. Thank you just didn't seem to be enough. "Well if you have the time and don't mind I would love that."

He looked at me with a serious expression. "Now not all people out here are like me." It didn't matter to me about everybody else. I had found a savior literally in my own back yard.

As I got up and headed for the kitchen, "Look it's getting late. The kids will have me up bright and early in the morning so I really need to get some sleep. Well, try to anyway. I haven't slept well since the accident."

Why the hell did I tell him that? That was none of his business.

He looked disappointed. "Well I told Charlie I would be here in the morning. What time do you think I should come by? Should I bring breakfast?"

My heart was screaming *don't go, Stay with me* but I couldn't give in to that temptation. After all we just met several hours earlier and I had made it clear I wasn't like that. "Well, they are usually up around seven so if you want to come by then you're welcome to. Don't bring breakfast though, I'll be cooking."

He started laughing. "You really do love to cook don't you?"

I chuckled. "Yeah I guess I do. It takes my mind off things." I hesitated, "I tell you what, it's really late and you probably won't be up by the time the kids get up so why don't you just come by when you get up."

What came next made my knees go weak. "Sweetheart," *he called me sweetheart? Did I hear that right?* "I work such odd hours I'm up when I need to be. If you want me here at seven then that's where I will be."

"Okay, if you're sure." as we walked to the door I stopped. "I'll tell you what. Don't take this the wrong way, but you are welcome to stay here tonight, on the couch of course. Then you can sleep till the kids get up."

He looked awestruck. "Well if you really don't mind I guess I could. I didn't expect that at all," he said laughing.

I went to get him a blanket and pillow. "I hope this blanket will be…"

I lost my train of thought at the sight of him without a shirt on sitting on my couch, his tan muscles rippling over his chest and arms. All I could think was *be strong, you have to stay strong; don't let it get to you.* Although it did get to me I think I hid it quite well.

"I hope this blanket will be heavy enough. I haven't figured out how to work this fancy air conditioner yet so I can't adjust the thermostat. If it's not just knock on my door and I will get you another one." I know he noticed me checking him out, but I was determined to be strong.

"Do you want me to take a look at it? I'm good with fancy things."

"No, that's ok. It's late. We will worry with it tomorrow. Try to get some sleep." He started walking towards me. I put my hand out to stop him and it landed on his chest. His muscles were so firm. They felt as good as they looked. *Close your mouth and look in his eyes* I had to tell myself. "I meant on the couch."

He stopped. "You really think I want something from you don't you?" I just stood there trying not to stare at his chest. "I do want something from you actually," as he started closer again. *There it was. Nobody ever wants something for nothing.* He leaned over and kissed me on the cheek, "I want you to get a good night sleep, sweetheart." He turned back to the couch. As he got comfortable I quickly went to my room before I did something I was going to regret.

As I lay in the bed I started to cry just thinking about the future without Jonathan. I kept reliving the accident over and over as I did so many nights. I was trying to be quiet. The last thing I wanted was for Michael to hear me cry myself to sleep. How was I going to raise these kids all by myself? Was I ever going to find someone with whom I had a connection like Jonathan? Just then there was a tap at my door.

Chapter 2

I quickly dried my eyes. "Come in." As the door opened, there was Michael.

"Are you ok?"

I tried to look as normal as possible. "Yes I'm fine. Did you need another blanket?"

As I got up to go get him another blanket he grabbed me. "No I don't need another blanket. The temperature is fine. There is something I do need though." He headed towards the bed. As he sat down I felt my defenses diminishing. "I need you to come sit right here." he patted the bed next to him.

"Look, I'm trying to be nice about this….."

As I was saying this he started smiling. "Would you just do me one favor? I know you don't know me, but would you just trust me? Only till morning then you can distrust me if you want." It seemed like a sensible request. I walked over and sat on the bed next to him. "Okay so we agree you're not going to freak out on me again? You're going to trust me till morning?" he asked, smiling.

"Yes we agree. No funny stuff though because one wrong move and I won't wait till morning to distrust you. Deal?"

He reached his hand out to shake mine "Deal." we sat there looking into each other's eyes. I could feel myself melting at the sight of him. He pulled back the blankets on my bed and patted my pillow. "Lay down please." I looked at him puzzled but did as he instructed. He lay down next to me and pulled the blankets over the both of us. "Put your head here," he instructed as he patted his chest. All I could think was that was really not a good idea, but I did as he asked. He put his arms around me, stroked my hair and kissed my forehead. "I always sleep better when I have someone with me. I know you're having a rough time. I hope this helps."

It must have because when I opened my eyes again it was morning. As I sat up I realized I was in bed all alone. Surely I hadn't dreamt it all. The clock in my room read ten o'clock. How could I have slept so late? The kids must be driving Steph crazy wondering what we were going to do today. The house seemed eerily quiet. I figured Steph had taken the kids outside to let me sleep. I went in the bathroom to wash my face and on the mirror is a message written in lipstick. *Hope you slept well. If we aren't outside check the kitchen.* It didn't look like Steph's writing, but who else could it have been?

Figuring Steph had the kids under control I went straight for the kitchen. There on the counter was an omelet with another note. *Sorry if it's not the way you like it, but I tried.* How sweet for Steph to cook me breakfast and deal with the kids so I could get some much needed rest. Breakfast on the patio seems to be the perfect, peaceful morning. I opened the door and heard "Mom!!!" all three yelled in unison.

Constance ran up to me and gave me a big hug, "Mom, we are so glad you're awake. We have the day all planned out already."

Oh no. what have they volunteered me for now? As I looked around I realized Steph is nowhere to be found. "Constance, where is Steph?"

She looked at me crazy and said, "Duh, mom! Michael gave her the day to herself."

I almost jumped out of my skin when someone grabbed me from behind. "I hope you don't mind. I got the kids breakfast." He grinned real big. "Made it myself. I also gave Steph a day to herself. We won't need her for what we are going to do today." So it wasn't a dream after all. He kissed me on the forehead. "Good morning sweetheart."

Standing there stunned all I could get to come out of my mouth was, "Thank you." I sat down to eat my breakfast as the kids fill me in on the big day they have all planned for us. Constance and Drew were really excited because Michael has promised to take them to the studio. Charlie, who is normally locked in his room, is running around like a normal child. He seems just as excited as the other two about the day's events.

"Mom," Charlie said, "Mr. Michael said he would be here this morning and he was!" He was acting like it was such a big deal but I could tell how much it meant to Charlie that someone did what they said they would.

"The limo will be here around eleven to get us," said Michael, quickly adding, "Can you be ready to go by then or should I call and change the time?"

I can't believe this is all happening. We are in California one day and now we are riding around in limos and hanging out with sexy, big movie stars? All I can think is things can only get better from here.

We arrive at the studio around lunch time.

"The first person you need to meet is the owner of the studio," Michael told Constance. "He will be the one that will help you get where you need to be in your career, provided you put in the work of course. His name is Mr. James. Our appointment is at one so we will grab something to eat first."

Walking around the studio the kids and I were in awe of everything it takes to make the shows you see on TV. Constance couldn't keep still for all the excitement. While walking along I heard that infamous shrill again. Constance started screaming, "Mom, Mom, Mom!" She is about to pull my clothes off when I look up and realize what she is freaking out over.

"Constance, calm down. What is the big deal?"

Michael asked. Apparently he thinks he is the only movie star these kids have eyes for. She was jumping up and down, trying to catch her breath to speak, but it's too late.

"Hey Michael. Who is this?" Donovan Weston asked. Donovan Weston is the star of "A Mary Movie", which is the kids' favorite movie. Next to Donovan Weston, Michael Stargate is chopped liver as far as these kids are concerned. Michael turned to introduce everyone, but only saw me. All three kids are hidden behind me at this point playing shy.

"Constance, come here. You can't run and hide every time you see a star. You won't get anywhere in this business." Michael reached out his hand. Constance shyly took it and eased out from behind me. The other two however were not moving. "Constance, this is-"

She interrupted him "I know who he is. He is in 'A Mary Movie' and it's my favorite."

Michael looked at her shocked, "I thought 'The Day the Stars Fell' was your favorite."

She looked at Michael disgusted, "It is, but 'A Mary Movie' is my all-time favorite. I watch it every day." Michael looked a little hurt, but Constance didn't notice. She was trying to muster everything she could to talk to Donovan. Donovan bent down and took her hand.

"So you're Constance right? It's nice to meet you. What brings you here?"

The shyness quickly dissipated and Constance's attitude quickly took over, "Well Michael's limo, DUH!"

I grabbed her, "Constance that wasn't very nice. Use your manners."

With that Donovan's eyes turned to me. "Constance, she is right. You should always use your manners. A person with good manners introduces people they know to each other." he said as he let go of her hand to take mine, giving Michael a dirty look. "Constance, if

22

you're going to be a big star in this town then you need to get used to showing off your family. I'm assuming this is your sister," he said looking at me. I blushed as I looked up at him. He had to be over six feet tall and looked much better in person than on the TV.

Before I could introduce myself Charlie peeked out from behind me. "That's not our sister, that's our mom and she likes Michael!" I didn't know where to hide I was so embarrassed. I quickly let go of Donovan's hand and grabbed Charlie.

As I was turning around to take care of Charlie, Donovan turned to Constance, "It was very nice to meet you and your mom. I hope to see you again sometime."

I was getting on to Charlie for being so rude when I noticed Donovan pull Michael to the side. It appeared the discussion got heated and although I couldn't hear the conversation I couldn't help but hear Donovan's parting words, "You better watch yourself Michael. I better not hear of it or you'll be sorry!" With that Donovan left.

What was that all about? Probably just some show biz stuff. I'm sure it's nothing for me to worry about. Yet I can't seem to just forget about it.

"Mom," shouted Constance, "Isn't he awesome? He is so cute and did you see how nice he was to me?"

I opened my mouth to speak but Michael cut me off, "Constance, there is something you should know about him. He isn't who he seems to be. He is one of the famous strangers your mom warned you not to talk to."

I can see the tears filling her eyes. She turned and looked at me. "I don't know him Constance so I don't know but Michael has been nothing but nice to us so I would listen to him." That explained Donovan's parting words. He was warning Michael not to tell us the truth about him. "Michael is there somewhere we can talk?" I asked.

"Sure. We can go to Mr. James's office. He has a playroom the kids will love." True to his word there are video games, ball pits, jungle gyms, and ride-on-toys in the office. The kids are in heaven.

"Michael, what was all that about with Donovan? He seemed pretty upset and then what you told Constance. I understand if you think he is a bad person, but you didn't have to be so blunt when telling her."

He looked at me stunned. "I'm sorry, Sherri. You just strike me as the type that doesn't lie to their children. I just don't want Constance to think that he is great because he really isn't."

I kind of smiled. "Michael are you sure you're not just trying to make sure you're the only star in her life?"

He leaned over and whispered in my ear, "I don't care about being the only star in her life. I want to be the only star in her mom's life." Before I could say anything he puts his lips to mine and gives me a kiss that made my knees go weak.

"Oooh Mama!" I turn around to see Charlie. I'm positive at that moment I was three shades of red.

"What is it Charlie?"

He walked over and hugged me. "Mom it's ok. I like Michael so you can kiss him." Michael and I looked at each other smiling.

"Constance," Mr. James's assistant calls. We walk in to a room as big as a school gym with awards everywhere.

"Hi there Constance. I'm Mr. Elroy James and I have been told you want to be a star."

Constance held her head high and walked over to him, "Hi Mr. Elroy James. Yes I do want to be a star. Mr. Michael says you can help me with that but I have to work hard."

Mr. James smiled at her. "You can call me Mr.

James and yes I can help you as long as you want to work hard. Can you sing Constance?"

From behind me I heard Drew yelling, "I can, I can, I can!"

Constance gave him a dirty look, "Drew, he wasn't talking to you!!" She turned her attention back to Mr. James, "Yes I can sing, but I love to play the guitar."

"Well Constance, you know it just happens that I have a guitar right over there."

She walked to the guitar but hesitated, "May I play it please?"

Mr. James looked at me, "You have a very polite young lady here. Is she always like this?"

Michael decided to answer for me, "Yes, from what I have seen she is. She would be a hit with the younger fans and a great role model."

Constance is next to the guitar wanting to touch it, but keeping her hands to herself very impatiently. Finally Mr. James gave her the ok. "So what are you going to sing for us today?" he asked.

She looked at him puzzled, "It doesn't really have a name, but I think you will like it." She starts to sing and Mr. James was obviously mesmerized. He pulled up a chair and sat staring at her like he had seen a ghost. When she finished he tried to regain his composure.

"I have never heard that song. Who wrote it?"

Constance was obviously starting to get upset. "You didn't like it? I can sing another one, I have a bunch."

He put his hand on her shoulder, "No, I loved it and you sang it beautifully. It looks like your mom has a talent for writing songs. The two of you could be the next Billy ray and Miley."

Disgusted she said, "Mr. James, I'm not meaning to be rude, but my mom didn't write that song, I did." Mr. James looked at me and I nodded to him that she is telling the truth. His mouth is open, but there are no words coming out. I looked at Michael and he shrugged his shoulders, not sure about what is happening either.

He looked at Constance, "Well I will tell you, I haven't seen anything like you in a long time. I would be honored to help walk you through the steps of getting your career started. Why don't you and your brothers wait in the play room while I discuss the details with your mother?" She screamed, started jumping up and down, and in a flash the three of them were gone.

We all sat down at Mr. James's desk. "Well you have quite a prodigy on your hands here. She plays guitar, sings, and writes her own songs. How old is she again?"

I was beaming with pride, "She will be nine very soon."

"Well Sherri, I'll be honest with you, even with her talent it's going to be a long and hard road but I believe she has the talent to make it if she can deal with the strain of the job."

"I-" as I started to speak I was interrupted by Michael.

"Mr. James, I have talked to her and explained how hard the job is and can be and she is willing and ready. That is the only reason I wanted you to see her. I would not have wasted your time if it wasn't going to be worth it to you."

The way he talked is almost like he wanted the credit for finding her. *No, that can't be. I'm just imagining things. He has been so good to us and given me no reason to doubt his intentions.*

"Sherri?" Mr. James was speaking to me, but I was zoning and didn't hear him, "Sherri?"

"Yes? I'm sorry. I'm just in awe of all of this. What were you saying?"

"The steps it's going to take to get her going. It's going to be a long and tedious road but I think we can make it as long as she doesn't give up."

I smiled knowing the next question out of my mouth would make me look stupid, "Can you outline the steps for me so I know what we are dealing with?"

"Well, the first thing we need to do Sherri is copyright all of her music. People will steal anything that they can in this city."

I stopped him, "We already did that. Anytime she writes a new song we immediately copyright it."

He looked at me shocked, "Well that's great. It looks like you're going to make a great manager for your daughter. You know more than you think you do about the business apparently."

Michael stepped in, "I will probably be managing her Mr. James, with the help of her mother, of course." I don't want to sound unappreciative or undermine him in front of his boss, but when we go outside I will be giving him a piece of my mind!

Mr. James turned his attention back to me, "As I was saying, since you already have the first step down then our next step will be getting her in the studio to record. We need to get her music ready for publishing. Once we have a CD ready to put together we will need to showcase her talent. Possibly a large party. This will accomplish two goals - we can make sure she will be able to handle singing in front of big crowds and also other talent can see her and we can find someone for her to tour with."

I interrupted, "A tour? Already? Isn't that a bit much for a child?"

He smiled, "Well if she isn't going to be able to take the pressure we can find out early. Once she does a tour her name and music will be out there. I will personally see to it that every radio station in the country has a copy on hand so that when people request it they will already have it. If all goes well when she returns from tour we will

27

go back in the studios and record her smash hit CD. After that it's all superstardom from there as long as she keeps her image clean."

I am so proud I could cry. "Oh trust me; I will NOT let her image get tarnished. I don't want this going to her head."

Mr. James explained he would have the papers drawn up and sent to me for my lawyer to look over. *My lawyer? I don't have a lawyer. Guess that better be the first thing I do.* We shake hands and are off to finish our day.

Constance asked a hundred questions in the ten minutes it took to get to the limo. She is so excited and I'm really excited for her. "Well Mr. James will have the papers sent to the house when he gets them drawn up. What was our next stop?" Michael says smiling at the kids.

"DISNEYLAND," they yell.

I haven't forgotten about the conversation I am going to have with Michael, but we just got great news so I will let it slide until we are alone and then bring it up. We spend the rest of the day at Disneyland.

Chapter 3

We walk in the house exhausted beyond belief. "Hey guys!" Steph hollers from the kitchen, "I cooked dinner."

Constance found her second wind and went running in the kitchen, "Steph, Steph, Steph! Guess what, guess what?"

Steph laughed at her, "You looked wore out when you came in the door. What could have given you this much energy?"

Constance started dancing around the kitchen, "I'm going to be a super star!!!"

Steph looked at me smiling, "I know. I was here when the papers were delivered and I hope you don't mind but the curiosity was killing me."

"No, I don't mind. I would have called you, but we have been at Disneyland all day."

After dinner Michael offered to put the kids to bed again. Sitting on the couch, my head still reeling from the last two days I want to talk to Michael about his behavior today, but I'm just too exhausted. It wasn't life threatening so I decided it could wait.

"The kids are in bed. I guess I'm going to go."

As I sat there looking at him I can't decide what I should say or do. Do I ask him to stay again? Do I let him leave? I was apparently staring off into space and his touch made me jump.

"I'm sorry. I didn't mean to startle you. Are you okay? You haven't seemed yourself today, just from the little I know of you, I mean."

I put my head in my hands, "It's just so much to take in right now. Things are happening a lot faster than I thought they would."

He put his arms around me, "I know it's a lot and to tell the truth I never expected it either. I don't want to put any pressure on you. I know your still struggling with your husband's death and I will always respect that, but you have to know that I want what's best for you and the kids. I want all of you to be happy. I have to admit, I haven't been this happy in a very long time and I have you and your kids to thank for that. I meant what I said in Mr. James's office today. You're the only star I need."

Was he really sitting here telling me he wanted to be with my kids and me? I have known him for two days and he was practically proposing. I look up at him with my jaw on the floor, "I.....I was talking about Constance and her career."

He turned what had to be five shades of red and stood up "I'm so sorry. I have to go."

He turned and hurried toward the door but I grabbed his arm and stopped him. "You can't leave like this. Please come sit down and let's talk about this." I don't know what to say, but I can't let him walk out of here embarrassed by what just happened. We walk back to the couch and sit down. Neither of us wants to be the first to speak, but I figure I should be the one. "Look Michael, I don't know you that well, but I do know how you make me feel and how my kids feel about you. That makes a lot of difference. You are the first man I have been attracted to since Jonathan died and that scares me. I can't sit here and say I haven't given any thought to us being US, but at the same time we live two different lives and I just don't know how it would work. I appreciate all the hard work your willing to give for my daughter but I don't want you to do it under false pretenses."

He took my hand, "Sherri, if you and I were together we could make it work, but even if we aren't I will not turn my back on your daughter or either of the other two. I told Constance I would help her and that's what I intend to do regardless of our situation." He started giggling, "We have made it work the last two days, haven't we?"

I can't believe he is joking about this, but it's a lot better than the awkwardness between us just minutes ago. "Only because you have put your life on hold to be with us. Michael it's not fair to you. You can't just give up YOUR dreams to make ours come true. I won't allow it."

He took my face in his hands and kissed me on the forehead then both cheeks. "Sherri, you don't need to worry about me. If I want to sacrifice my career to take care of you guys then that's what I will do, with or without your consent." He paused and seemed to consider what he just said, "Look, that sounded harsh and I'm sorry, but what you don't understand is I never wanted this career in the first place, it was forced on me by my parents. Your daughter has real talent and I don't want anyone to take advantage of her. That is why I told Mr. James I would be her manager. I wasn't trying to step on your toes, but you're new to the scene and the sharks around here will eat you alive if they have a hint that you don't know what you're doing. If we tell everyone I'm her manager then they will leave her alone. I wanted to talk to you about all of this before but I never found the right time. I hope I didn't overstep my boundaries."

I felt so stupid. I was ready to chew his head off and once again all he was trying to do was help. "I just hope I'm not pushing her into this. I don't want her to look back and realize she gave up her childhood for money. I have always taught my kids that money doesn't buy happiness-"

Before I could finish he put his finger to my lips, "The difference is Constance has so much talent. If the singing becomes too much for her she can always just write for the big name stars. I don't know of anyone around here

31

that isn't going to die when they hear her music. Don't worry. She will be fine. I will see to it if you will let me." He has a way that always makes me feel so at peace. "Well, I'm going to go, unless you want me to stay," he said as he got up.

I don't know what I want him to do. My head is in a million places right now. I knew things moved fast here, but never realized how fast. I took his hand. "Do you think you can be a good boy tonight?"

He started laughing. "Sweetheart, nothing will happen unless you want it to happen, this I promise you." He laughed even harder, "Hey it's your world, I'm just a squirrel." We both laughed.

"Let's go to bed then. Charlie will want you here when he gets up in the morning."

The sun was up before I knew it. Getting up out of bed I realized the house was very quiet. I looked over and Michael was still sleeping. The kids were apparently very tired from their big adventure yesterday if they were still in bed. As I walked by the back door I heard the kids outside with Steph and another voice that sounded very familiar but I just couldn't place it.

I opened the door and saw Donovan standing there with only running shorts and tennis shoes on. I couldn't help but notice the sweat glistening on his finely tan body. He has the body of a god and you can see every muscle, his grey eyes sparkling in the sunlight. His light brown hair not moving at all. He had a more muscular body than Michael and there was nothing baby about his face. I couldn't help but stare deep in thought.

What is it with all these Hollywood guys? I was snapped back to reality when he spoke.

"Morning," he said, "I hope we didn't wake you. I was just talking to the kids about their adventure

32

yesterday." At this point I'm really not sure what to think. *Do these stars have nothing better to do than to show up on my doorstep every day?* "Your daughter was just telling me about her career. She seems very excited about it. If you need the name of a good lawyer or a manager for her I will be more than happy to help."

I felt an arm around my waist, "We have it under control. Thank you for your offer, but I think between the two of us we can handle it. Great seeing you again, Donovan. I think it's time for you to leave." Michael is being very rude, but trying to do it in a nice way. I hadn't seen this side of him other than when we ran into Donovan at the studio. There is some terrible tension between them. I just wish I knew what it was.

"Well, I'm sorry I intruded," Donovan said to me. He turned to Constance, "You keep up the good work. You will get where you want to be." Addressing Michael he said, "You better watch yourself. I meant what I said yesterday." We all watched as he jogged back to the beach.

I was so preoccupied yesterday that I had forgotten about their conversation at the studio lot. I wanted answers and I wanted them now. "Michael, what was that all about? Every time we run into him he threatens you."

Michael pulled me to the side. "It's not a conversation we need to have in front of the kids. Why don't you see if Steph will watch the kids while we go do all the legal stuff and I can tell you about it while we are out?"

We climbed in the limo.

"So?"

He started laughing. "It's killing you not to know isn't it?"

I don't find it funny at all. "Donovan doesn't sound like he is kidding when he threatens you and I don't want my kids hurt because of something that has nothing to do with them. You can either tell me what is going on or I can ask him."

He put his hands on my shoulders and turned me to face him, "Look, calm down. It's not as bad as it sounds. It goes way back actually. Donovan tends to hold a grudge. It all started with his girlfriend. About 3 years ago he was engaged to Amy Jones."

"The model?" I interrupted.

"Yes that's her. Anyway they were engaged and Amy decided to have one last fling before they got married. Unfortunately, I had been out of the country and had NO idea that they were getting married, so when she called me up I took her out. Donovan called off the wedding and he has been kind of stalking me ever since. He never even tried out for 'A Mary Movie' until he heard that I was going to get the lead and then he wanted to take something from me so he auditioned and got the part. I try not to hold it against him, but he is always in my face. Let's just keep our distance from him and everything will be fine."

Arriving at the lawyer's office I have butterflies in my stomach. I really hope I'm doing the right thing. Everything seemed to be going well as we sat down to sign the papers.

"Who is going to be her manager?" the lawyer asked.

Michael looks at me. "What do you want to do?"

I gave him the go ahead. With the papers all signed the lawyer started explaining the legal stuff to me. Michael's phone rang and he excused himself.

"Now everything is in order. Michael will be Constance's manager for at least a year. His contract is renewable after that if you wish. He will get fifteen percent of everything Constance makes."

I stopped him. "Fifteen percent? That could turn out

to be a lot of money."

The lawyer eased my mind as he explained, "Well he only wants fifteen percent. Most manager's take thirty percent so I was really shocked to hear him say only half of what everyone else gets."

I felt much more assured knowing that Michael only wanted fifteen percent as opposed to the thirty percent that most managers seek. I shook the lawyer's hand, thanked him for everything, and turned to leave. As I walked out of the lawyer's office I overheard Michael on the phone.

"I said I would be there. Will you chill out? I understand that and I will be there I promise. I have to go." He quickly hung up the phone.

"You have to go somewhere?" He grabbed my hand as we walked out of the building.

"Yeah, I have something I have to take care of. I can blow it off if you don't want me to go?" We got in the limo,

"Depends on what it is. Is it something important?"

He took my hand and looked into my eyes, "Nothing is more important to me than you guys, but there is a kid who has terminal cancer and his last wish is to meet me. I promised I would go, but I don't have to."

How could he think I would say no to that? I know he doesn't know me very well but I don't know anyone that would tell him not to go. "No, the kids and I can manage without you. You go do that for that poor kid. We will be here when you get back."

We returned home and shortly afterward he had to leave but reassured me saying, "I will be back as soon as I possibly can. Until then don't do anything without checking with me first. PLEASE be careful and above all else stay away from Donovan. If he did or tried anything with y'all to try to get back at me I would have to kill him."

We have a couple days until we start going to the

studio and with all the excitement I decided spending time at home would be a good idea. Michael wouldn't be back until Monday anyway so it gives me time to spend with the kids, just us. We haven't had that since we got here and after Monday I wasn't sure when we would again. A couple of days to lounge on the beach sounded like paradise right now.

I'm in the kitchen getting things ready for dinner when the doorbell rang. I opened the door to see Donovan standing there, this time fully dressed. "Hi, do you remember me?" he asked.

Michael was right. Donovan had to be stalking him. Michael hadn't been gone ten minutes before Donovan showed up.

"I'm sorry Donovan. I'm not being rude, but I can't talk to you," and I closed the door. I felt really bad for shutting the door in his face. That was very rude of me, but I am not getting in the middle of their feud. It doesn't concern me or my children so I have no need for it.

"Sherri!!"

What the hell? How does he know my name? Not that it matters. Its drama and it doesn't concern my family so I don't need it. "Go away Donovan! I will call the cops."

I knew he was mad because he hit the door, "Sherri there are some things you need to know but I'll go. Just know that this isn't over."

Oh good grief! I have lived in my house two whole days and now I'm going to have to move again. I didn't sign up for all of this. I expected paparazzi when Constance or Drew became famous, but not stalker actors. I walked to the back door, "Steph, get the kids and get inside now!"

I sent the kids upstairs to the playroom while I filled Steph in on everything that has happened.

"Wow," she said, "that is just crazy no matter how you put it. What is his problem?"

I told her everything that Michael has told me. She looked at me puzzled. "You know, I know people in California are strange, but I didn't realize they were this strange. Are you sure you want to do this?"

I think long and hard before answering, "Yes. It's what the kids want and I'm an adult so I can stop all the drama not to mention Michael has assured me he won't let anything happen to us."

"Do you really trust Michael?" she asked.

"I don't completely trust him, but he has given me no reason not to. Until he does, I suppose I will trust him as much as I can let myself."

"So," she said grinning, "what's going on with you and Michael?"

I tell her all about everything that has happened over the last twenty-four hours.

"Wow. He is a great guy. It didn't take you long to find someone, did it?" she mused grinning from ear to ear.

"I wasn't really looking. He found me to be honest. It just kind of happened. I honestly don't know what to think about the whole situation."

Finally some much needed down time. The kids are in the bed and with nobody around but Steph so we settled in to watch a movie. I realized it was getting late and that I hadn't heard from Michael. No sooner than the thought flitted through my brain the phone rang.

"Hello?" I said into the receiver.

"Hey there sweetheart. How are you?"

I slouched down in the couch smiling. "I'm fine. How is your trip?"

"Well I may have to be here longer than I expected. I'm going to do my best to be back no later than Monday morning. If I don't get back you can get in touch with Mr. James and he can get you and Constance all set up in the studio."

Okay, this is so not what I wanted to hear. "Well you have to do what you have to do, but listen-" I said, trying to figure out how to tell him about Donovan.

"What is it sweetheart? Is everything ok?"

I scramble trying to figure out the best way to tell him without upsetting him. "Yes and no. We are fine, but you need to know that Donovan came by after you left."

"What?!? Came by where? What happened?"

I let out a sigh, "Calm down. He came by the house about ten minutes after you left."

"What did he want? Did you let him in? What did he say?"

He won't let me answer one question before he asks another one. "Michael, if you will calm down and let me speak I will tell you exactly what happened and what was said."

He got really quiet, "I'm sorry sweetheart. I didn't realize he was going to be this big of a problem. He normally keeps his distance. What happened?"

I gathered myself and proceeded to tell him, "He knocked and I didn't know who it was. When I opened the door and saw it was him I closed the door in his face. I told him I didn't want to talk to him. I threatened to call the cops. He said he was leaving but this wasn't over."

The line went quiet until Michael said "I need to go I will call you back." and abruptly hung up.

I stared at the receiver in my hand, "That was strange."

"Yeah, I heard him yelling over here. Is he ok?" Steph asked.

"Honestly Steph, I don't know. He practically hung up on me."

As I said that the phone rang again. I answered it thinking it would be Michael, "Hello sexy."

The voice on the other end says "Well hello yourself sexy."

What? Who the hell?

Chapter 4

"Who is this?" I asked.

"Look if I tell you who it is you will hang up."

They think they are cute huh? Well apparently they don't know me. "If you DON'T tell me who it is I will hang up."

There is a long pause and finally the voice on the other end said, "I will tell you if you promise not to hang up."

Being quick on my feet, "And if you don't tell me who this is I will hang up. So either way it looks like I'm hanging up."

I took the phone away from my ear and heard screaming. "Sherri! Please don't hang up. We really need to talk!"

I put the phone back up to my ear, "So are you ready to tell me who this is?" Silence again. "Look I don't make it a habit to play on the phone. I'm an adult and if you need to talk so bad then I suggest you tell me who you are or we have nothing to talk about."

After a brief pause the voice said, "I will tell you who this is, but I need to tell you that after I do you're going to hang up and there is something you really need to know."

By this point I have gotten pretty irritated. "Look either you tell me who this is or you don't, either way this conversation is over."

"I'm sorry Sherri; I'm not trying to play games. This is Donovan."

I sat there in amazement. *How dare he call this house! How did he even get my number? This guy is crazy!*

"Look Donovan I am hanging up now, but before I do I'm going to say two things to you. Do not interrupt me and listen to what I say carefully because I'm only saying it once. I have been warned about you and I want nothing to do with this drama-"

He tries to interrupt, "But-"

I stopped him, "But nothing! I said do not interrupt! I do not want nor need this drama and do not call this house again. Goodbye!"

I threw the phone across the couch.

"What was all that about?" Steph asked. Before I could even start to answer her the phone rang again. Steph picked it up and started to answer it,

"No," I said, "I've got this," and she handed me the phone.

I didn't even say hello this time, "I SAID DON'T CALL HERE AGAIN!!! ARE YOU DEAF OR JUST DUMB??"

"What? I said I would call you back. You didn't say not to. What is going on?" Michael sounded concerned.

"Look Michael, I don't know how much of this I can take. He didn't come back over here, but he called. He seems really adamant to tell me something. Is it really that big of a deal that I find out what his problem is or what he wants with me?"

Michael was silent for a minute, "Well if you really feel the need to talk to him I can't stop you, but all he wants is Constance."

I sat there wondering what my daughter had to do with this drama. "What are you talking about Michael?"

Michael sighed, "I didn't want to tell you this because I was trying to shield you from it, but when I told you the sharks would eat you alive...well he is one of the sharks. Everybody wants to get their hands on your daughter. Look, this is a conversation we need to have in person. If you want to talk to him you can. I would really rather you didn't, but if you really need to then just promise me you won't feed into his lies. I called my lawyer when I hung up a little bit ago and he is on his way over with papers for a restraining order. You can have him retype the papers where it says he is allowed around you if he is invited. If you don't want to do the restraining order you don't have to, but I was just trying to help cut out the drama."

His explanation made sense. Mr. James did say I had a prodigy on my hands and Michael had already warned me about everybody wanting a piece of the pie.

"Okay." I say.

"Okay what?" he said laughing.

"Okay I won't talk to him. We will deal with all of this when you get back. When the lawyer gets here I will have him retype the papers just in case I change my mind, but it's only to prevent any other drama."

Michael was really quiet, "Thank you sweetheart. We will talk about all of this when I get back, I promise. See you soon."

I just wanted a nice quiet night in my new house and the drama took over. I can't do this the rest of my life, especially when it supposedly has nothing to do with me. There is a knock at the door. I'm almost terrified to even see who it is, but I know Mr. Jackson is supposed to be on his way. As I opened the door I whispered to myself, "Please be Mr. Jackson. Please be Mr. Jackson." I hesitated as I grabbed the knob and finally got the confidence to open it.

"Hi Sherri." Thank goodness it's Mr. Jackson.

"Please come in. There has been a change of plans. Michael said we could change the paperwork to say that Donovan could come around me if he was invited. I think that's what I want to do. I'm not trying to hurt anyone's feelings or cause any more problems."

Mr. Jackson took out his cell phone. "If you will

42

excuse me I will have that taken care of right now."

How is he going to do that right here in my house?
We went inside as he is getting off the phone. "It won't
take long. My assistant is going to make the changes and
send it over by messenger. Are you sure this is what you
want?"

I must have been very hesitant. He put his hand on
my shoulder, "Look Sherri, if that is what you want then
we will do it, but you need to know that Donovan is a very
spoiled person and doesn't stop until he gets what he wants.
He is very persistent."

"I'm sure. I just need all of this to be over with so
that I can focus on my kids." I replied.

The messenger arrived with the new paperwork and
Mr. Jackson went over it with me. "Is there anything else
you need tonight Sherri?"

I let out a big sigh of relief. "No sir, I believe that
will take care of it. Thank you so much for working so late
to take care of this."

He chuckled. "That's why I make the big bucks.
You have a nice night and if you need anything just give
me a call."

With Mr. Jackson gone I might as well turn in for
the night. It seemed to be the only way I will get any peace
and quiet.

Up before dawn is never any fun but I am
determined that I will enjoy some peace and quiet this
morning if it kills me. While sitting drinking my morning
Dr. Pepper I realize I haven't checked the mail since we
moved in. It's still dark outside so if Donovan is out there I
will beat him to death with my baseball bat. I am sure not
going outside before daylight without protection, especially
with all the crazies that seem to be running around this
town. I grabbed the baseball bat and walked out to the

mailbox.

Junk mail, mail for the old residents, and an envelope with just my name on it. No return address, no stamp. *This wasn't mailed. Someone put it in my mailbox.* I'm pretty sure it was Donovan. *Should I open it?* I did tell Michael I wouldn't talk to him, but Donovan isn't here so technically it's not talking. It's a letter. He is determined to talk to me so I might as well, not to mention the curiosity is starting to reach its boiling point. I open the envelope and there is a single piece of notebook paper. I carefully pull it out and open it.

I'm not wasting any more time. I know everything you need to know. You know who this is. Contact me and you will be able to make your own decisions. Be careful, me.

Well the curiosity HAD reached a boiling point, but now it's completely boiled over. I knew who me was, but what was so important I needed to know? What made him think I wasn't making my own decisions? And how was I supposed to get in touch with him? He left no address, phone number, anything. But most importantly why did I need to be careful? This is going to drive me crazy all day if I don't find something to get my mind off of it.

What can we do today? Might as well do some shopping. All three kids need new clothes. The sun comes up and kids started to trickle out of bed. We ate breakfast, loaded up in the convertible, and headed to Rodeo Drive. We can't afford anything there but I have always wanted to go.

We are in and out of shops looking at overpriced clothes made by people we have never heard of, having a good time none the less, but I can't shake this feeling I'm being watched. If it's Donovan I'm going to talk to him. I'm going to find out what is going on. I feel like I'm in a horror movie and I'm going to be the next to die. The hair

44

on the back of my neck starts to stand up. I look around and spot him. It's Donovan, but he is 100 yards away which is what the restraining order says.

As I walk towards him he turned and walked away. I followed him to a parking garage. I have seen enough horror movies to know not to go in there after him. I just don't understand why he wouldn't stop to talk to me. What is his game? I walked back to Steph and the kids.

"What was that all about?" She asked.

"I don't have a clue, but it gives me the creeps. Maybe we should just go back to the house and hide there for a little while. I don't know what exactly is going on here, but I have a bad feeling about the whole thing." Steph agreed.

I tried to call Michael on the way home but he didn't answer his phone. I figured he would call me back as soon as he could. He is probably at the hospital still. I really hope he is coming home soon. I feel safer when he is here with us, even though I don't know why. It looks like Donovan is going to great lengths to keep me away from him. Money does strange things to people.

It's Monday and I have no choice but to drag myself out of bed. I know that I have to call Mr. James to see about the studio time because Michael was supposed to but he isn't answering his phone yet again. I haven't heard from him since Saturday night and I don't really know if I should be worried or not. I called Mr. James and he gave me directions and told me to talk to Jennifer and that she would take care of everything.

Constance and I head to the studio. Jennifer met us at the door.

"So," she says, "You must be our almost famous singer I have been hearing so much about." Constance smiled at her. "Constance we are going to record at least one song a day until we can fill up an album. Do you know how many songs it takes to fill up an album?"

Constance looked at her crazy. "What is an album? Is it the same thing as a cd?"

Jennifer laughed. "Well pretty much. We are going to have to record seventeen songs at least. Do you have that many songs?"

It was Constance's turn to laugh then. "Well Ms. Jennifer, I have a lot more than that. Can I pick the songs?"

Jennifer looks at her in amazement. "Mr. James wasn't kidding. Sure you can suga. Let's get started."

By Wednesday Constance has made remarkable progress. She is almost done with her first album. Words can hardly describe how proud I am of her.

I still haven't heard from Michael since he called Saturday night. I don't know what is going on with him and I'm beginning to get very upset. He is getting paid for all of this yet I'm doing the work. My phone rang while we were at the studio and jarred me from my musings.

"Hello?"

"Hey sweetheart." Well, well. Speak of the devil. I didn't say anything as I hadn't decided if I was still speaking to him.

"Sherri?"

I guess I might as well talk to him. He is getting paid regardless of our relationship and I'm really curious as to why I haven't heard from him.

"Yeah I'm here."

Hesitantly, he asked, "Is everything okay sweetheart?"

"Yes everything…actually no its not. Where have you been? Why am I doing this all by myself? I thought you were going to help me."

He started to cry. "The little kid that had cancer died and I wanted to go to the funeral. I'm so sorry I didn't call but I'm hoping you would understand."

Understand? What was I supposed to say to that? *Um no, I don't understand that you cared about some sick child*? That would be heartless.

"Sherri?"

What could I say? "Yeah Michael, I'm here. I'm sorry for getting so aggravated. I should have known you had a good reason for leaving me out to dry, so to speak. So when are you coming home?"

I felt an arm around my waist and an ever so gentle kiss on my neck. After the weekend we had had I turned around and slapped him. There, looking slightly amused and with a perfect imprint of my hand across his cheek, stood Michael.

"I said I was sorry sweetheart."

I threw my hands to my mouth, "OH MY GOODNESS!!! I am so sorry."

He laughed. "Well I guess I kind of deserved it. After all I didn't call you for several days." I kissed him on the cheek and we turned to watch Constance.

"How is she doing Jennifer?" Michael asked.

"She is doing great. We almost have a whole album already and we just started Monday." Jennifer patted Michael on the back and went in to talk to Constance.

It is so nice to have him back that I forgot all about the drama that went on while he was gone. I hadn't had any other problems so it had to be over with anyway. The album is finished and I couldn't be more proud. Constance is on top of the world. We have to go meet with Mr. James about the party.

"Constance, Mr. James will see you now," his assistant called.

"Hi Mr. James, do you want me to sing for you again?" Constance asks.

Mr. James smiled at her. "No honey. We are here to

talk about your party. Are you going to be able to sing in front of a bunch of people?"

Constance gets a smug look on her face, "I can sing in front of millions!" We all laugh.

"Well," Mr. James said, "We are going to start a little bit smaller than that. We are going to shoot for about one hundred people. Do you think that would be okay Constance?"

Beaming with pride she responds, "That would be no problem Mr. James."

Mr. James turned his attention to Michael, "So what I need you to do is handle everything but the guest list. I will take care of that. You have been to Hollywood parties and you know how it works. Let's make it happen. Give me a date and time and we will get it going."

Michael looked at me. "I don't know what all we need to do so don't look at me," I said chuckling.

"Well," Michael started thinking out loud, "We need to book the caterer, line up the bar, and find a place."

Constance jumped in, "We can do it at our house, and what's a caterer?"

Michael put his arm around her, "Sweetie a caterer is someone that cooks food."

Constance jumped in my lap, "That would be my mom," she said.

"I guess I could cook if you wanted me to darling," I said.

"Okay I guess we just need a date and time."

Michael looked at me again. "Well I guess the real question is how long it will take for you to get food ready for one hundred people."

I laughed at the thought. "I can have it done tonight."

Mr. James thought about that for a minute. "How about we aim for Monday night. That is four days so

48

everyone will have plenty of notice." We all agree and
Constance thanked Mr. James again.

When we walked in the house, Charlie comes
running and screaming, "MR. MICHAEL, MR.
MICHAEL! I'M SO GLAD YOUR BACK!!! I MISSED
YOU SO MUCH!!!" He jumped and Michael picked him
up.
　　　"I missed you to man. Did you hold down the fort
while I was gone?" Charlie nodded. "Well you don't have
to worry. I'm not going anywhere for a long time so I will
be right here. We have a big party coming up and I'm
going to need your help to get everything together. Can you
help me?" Again Charlie nodded.
　　　The kids missed Michael almost as much as I did so
after dinner we decided to all watch a movie together. Two
hours later the kids are asleep all over the living room and
Michael picks them up one at a time and puts them in bed.
　　　"They are down for the count," he said sitting next
to me on the couch. He put his arm around my shoulders
and pulled me to him. I just want to stay here forever. "You
know sweetheart," Michael starts, "We won't have a lot of
time after Constance is picked up to go on tour, so I was
thinking…" He turned me to face him. "What if you and I
went on a trip?" I started to interrupt but he stopped me, "I
know we have a ton to do, but I was thinking just for the
day, just you and I. What do you think?"
　　　What do I think? I don't know what to think. I think
it would be amazing, but I just really don't have time. I
have so much to do. "Honestly, Michael, I need to make
sure everything is perfect for this party. I don't do anything
without putting myself all into it."
　　　He looked disappointed. "Okay, hear me out and
then you can make up your mind. We can go tomorrow.
Leave first thing in the morning and be back before

midnight. Just say you will think about it."

I wanted to. Oh, how I wanted to, but I had so much to do for the party and I couldn't just dump the kids on Steph again. "I will think about it. I don't feel right leaving the kids with Steph so much."

He smiled. "I already cleared it with Steph. She is going to take care of the kids and I hired a maid and decorator to come in and take care of the house. All you have to do is take care of the food and then go Monday and get a new dress and have a spa day with Constance and Steph while I take the boys. I have it all set up. I just need you to say yes."

How can I say no now? He had gone through all this trouble just for me. I gave him a small kiss on the lips, "Yes, but you have to promise we will be home in time for me to get everything done. This is very important to me and I will not let my daughter down."

He jumped up and headed for the door, "Better get packed. We leave in the morning."

I stood up, "Wait, where are we going? What are we doing?"

He smiled and said, "Dress comfortable is all I'm going to tell you. The limo will pick us up at five in the morning. I'm going to run home and get packed myself and I will see you in the morning." With a quick kiss he was out the door.

I packed and went to bed hoping I would be able to sleep with all the excitement going on.

I wake to a gentle kiss on my neck. *Hmmm.* "Wake up sweetheart. The limo will be here shortly and we have to get going."

In the limo I can't stand the anticipation, "Please tell me where we are going."

He smiled, "I can't do that, because if I do then you

50

might change your mind. You will have a good time I promise."

We boarded a private jet and were in the air as the sun came up. "You really aren't going to tell me anything?" I half asked, half stated.

He looked at me with a self-righteous smirk on his face and answered, "All I'm going to say is if you aren't pleased I will be very disappointed. It's not a long flight so you won't have long to be curious."

I just sat back and stared out the window with my thoughts all over the place. We landed in a familiar place that I knew all too well, New Orleans, La. As we got off the plane there was a limo waiting for us.

I turned to Michael, "What are you up to?"

He just smiled and offered his hand to help me off the plane. Once in the limo he instructed the driver, "To the house by way of the route I already gave you."

With that we were off.

"Michael, I really think you need to at least give me a hint what you're up to. Do you own a house out here or something? You're really making me nervous."

He could see the concern in my eyes and decided to come clean. "Honestly, Sherri, I don't own a house here. This is not the end of our journey. After your story about your husband I could see how much you loved him and I wanted to share that with you."

Puzzled I said, "Michael, what are you talking about? I don't understand what you're saying. You're not making any sense."

He took my hand and kissed me on the forehead. "Sweetheart, there is no way I can explain it so that you will understand, so just sit back and relax. We will be there shortly."

The partition came down and the driver announced, "Sir, we are almost at Main Street as you requested."

I felt the car turn a corner and stop. I heard a loud roaring outside but couldn't see because of the tint on the windows.

Michael leaned over, "The wait is over, sweetheart." He rolled down my window. Main Street was lined with people cheering and clapping. I realized we were back in Houma.

I turned to him. "Michael, what is this?"

He smiled. "It's a parade for us. I hope you like it."

I was so shocked I couldn't do or say anything. Finally I found my voice, "But Michael, why are they cheering us? I mean I know you're famous but Constance hasn't even started yet so I don't understand why they would be cheering for me."

He kissed me ever so gently. "You will understand in just a minute."

The car stopped and we stepped out into town square. There in front of me was a life size statue of Jonathan and the other men that were from Houma killed with him. The mayor stood on a podium and quieted the crowd.

"And now for our very own hometown hero and the founder of 'Make a Child's Dream Come True,' please help me welcome Sherri," the Mayor said.

Shock overtook me and I couldn't move. Michael took my hand and whispered, "Sherri, we have to go say something. I will do all the talking."

I shot him a look. "Well, I would hope so since I don't have a clue what's going on."

I shook as I walked up to the podium. Michael got everyone quiet once again and took the microphone. "Thank you everyone for being here. I will keep this short. It's a true honor to see you all and be able to see where Sherri comes from. This monument is here to remind each and every one of you that life is too short and you should never take anything for granted. Sherri knows all too well how life can change in an instant. The foundation has been set up so that every child has the opportunities to live their dreams no matter what the cost. Anyone interested in the program should see the Mayor's office for full details. Thank you for your time and support."

Michael took my hand. "Come sweetheart, it's time for the last part of our journey."

I was still visibly shaken but tried to smile and wave as we got back in the limo with everyone cheering and clapping. Once in the car and out of the public view I turned to him, "What did you do?"

He looked at me upset and asked, "You didn't like it?"

At a loss for words I said, "Honestly Michael, I'm still not sure what just happened so I have no idea."

He smiled gently and explained that my story inspired him so he started a charity in my hometown in my name and had the statue built to remind people of what is really important in life. I started crying. He wrapped me tightly in his arms apologizing profusely. The car stopped again and he told the driver to give us a minute before letting us out.

He turned to me, "Sherri, I wasn't trying to hurt you." The tears started to well up in his eyes. "That is the last thing on this earth I wanted to do. I just wanted to help you honor the love of your life."

Tears were streaming down both our faces. I reached over and wiped a tear from his cheek. "Oh, Michael. Honestly, I'm not upset. I can't believe you did all of this for us and for him."

I threw my arms around him but he pulled back, "So you forgive me? You're not upset?"

I smiled through the tears. "There is nothing to be forgiven for. Although a little heads up next time might be sufficient."

We both laughed. He knocked on the window signaling the driver to let us out. As the door opened I saw a beautiful house I had seen many times before – an old white plantation house with columns running along the front. They had turned this particular one into a bed and breakfast further back than I could remember. Jonathan and I had spent our honeymoon here. It was surrounded by woods and had a large beautiful gazebo overlooking an orchard of rose bushes of every color imaginable.

I turned to him, "Well, Michael, it's so nice you don't mind staying with all the 'common folk'." We both laughed as we walked toward the house.

As we walked in the front door I realized it wasn't like I remembered at all. It was beautifully decorated with a congratulations banner hanging in the foyer. The same little old lady was still running the place after all this time. "Hello Mr. Stargate. Welcome. Your room is ready."

He thanked her and took the key. "Is everything as I asked for?"

"Yes, sir," she answered smiling. "Dinner is promptly at five."

He returned her smile and we went upstairs. Once in the room he turned to me and kissed me. "Sweetheart, why don't you relax in a bubble bath? I have a few more things to take care of."

With that he left me to relax.

As I soaked in my bubble bath I let my mind wander. I couldn't believe the day's events. I replayed everything over in my mind again but my thoughts were interrupted, "Sweetheart, we have to be down for dinner shortly."

I quickly finished my bath and dressed for the evening. We went downstairs and there was an intimate dinner for two prepared. As we ate I saw an opportunity to talk about the day. "Michael, I really want to thank you for today. It has been amazing."

He took my hand and said, "Well sweetheart, it's not over. Please come with me."

He handed me a single long stem red rose and lead me to the door that led out to the gazebo. As he opened the door I heard "SURPRISE!" and I looked around and saw so many familiar faces - Mrs. Rosa and Mr. Jacob, Jonathan's parents, Steph's boyfriend, Steve, Theresa, my mother who I haven't spoken to since the accident, and a lot of people I went to high school with.

It looks like he has tried to put together a list of people who were closest to me. I no longer had anything to do with anyone but Mrs. Rosa, Mr. Jacob, and Steve. The rest of them, including my mom, thought I was crazy for taking the kids to California. He really had no way of knowing and I couldn't fault him for that.

I looked around and smiled, noticing that nobody was trying to approach me, which I found slightly odd. Michael turned to me, "This way, sweetheart."

"Michael, what's going on here?"

He led me to the middle of the gazebo and turned to me. "Sherri, the last few days have made me realize what I want out of life. I have never been happier and I don't ever want to lose this feeling." He backed up and knelt down on one knee.

Chapter 5

I swear I almost fainted. *OMG!! Surely he wasn't going to propose. There's no way. We haven't known each other long enough to get married.*

He pulled the ring out of his pocket, "Sherri, I know you think this is where your life ended when you lost Jonathan, but I'm here to show you and all your friends and family that this is where your life begins. I'm asking you to marry me, but before you say no, hear me out. I'm not doing this because I want to get married tomorrow or even next week. I know I have found what I want for the rest of my life. I know you're not sure and I expect you to say no, but if you will listen to me, I think you will find what I say makes sense. The last few days have been like heaven to me, and if I didn't try I would hate myself forever for letting you get away. I'm asking you to marry me in a year or two when you have had time to realize what I already know. If you say no then nothing changes, but if you say yes I promise not to pressure you in any way. Please at least say you will consider it."

I was flabbergasted and didn't have a clue what to say. My heart was saying go for it but my head was telling me he had lost his mind. "Why should I marry you?" I asked.

"I am crazy about you and I know I have found my soul mate. I know you think Jonathan was your soul mate and he may have been but I want to show you that I can be the love of your life. I will never try to take his place in your heart. I would just like for you to make space in there for me," he replied. "And I just can't pass up the opportunity before our lives get hectic to try and make you mine."

I looked into his eyes and my heart melted. "But

Michael, I don't plan on leaving you. Why make this big of a step right now?"

His eyes filled with tears. "Sherri, I have learned to live each day like there is no tomorrow. I thought with the accident maybe you had the same feeling. Things move very fast in California and I don't want to become a statistic by jumping into something, but I also don't want to let you get away. You are everything I have ever wanted in a woman and I can't let that go."

"You promise to give me time? We won't get married right away, right?" I asked.

He smiled. "I promise. I just want a promise from you that you will be all mine and when the time is right we will make it official."

I heard everyone muttering under their breath things like, "She should really say yes," and "This kind of stuff only happens in the movies."

I looked over at Jonathan's parents and Mrs. Rosa gave me a smile and a nod.

"This is such a big step, and I know I'm crazy for doing this, but YES!"

Everyone cheered and started hugging me and shaking his hand.

My mom walked over to me and hugged me. "It's so good to see you. You look like you're doing well. How are the kids?"

Before I could say anything the same disapproving, condescending mother I had always known showed her face, "You know you are a fool if you think this won't end badly. I hope for the kid's sake you know what you're doing."

Luckily Michael saved me. "Sweetheart, I hate to do this to you, but we have to get back on the jet if we are going to make it home before midnight."

He introduced himself to Theresa and she just

turned and walked off.

Upon arriving home everyone was up waiting for us. "SO…" Steph asks looking at Michael.

"She said…YES!!!" The kids started jumping up and down cheering.

"So you had this all planned out already?" I asked giving him a glance.

"Yeah, he asked me about it yesterday. I thought you would say no for sure though," Steph admitted.

"We aren't getting married anytime soon. I said I would one day, Not tomorrow or anything," I assured them smiling.

"I have to go home tonight, sweetheart. I will be back first thing in the morning so we can get everything going for the party though," Michael said kissing me. "I love you."

I love you? That sounded so strange coming from a man other than Jonathan. It sounds even weirder coming out of my mouth.

"I love you to. See you in the morning."

When I wake up the next morning reality sets in and I have a million things to do. I still have to go grocery shopping to get what I need for the party. I look down at my finger thinking it had all been a dream. The only dream is the size of the ring I am wearing. I can't believe that a super star wants to marry me. This is the kind of stuff that only happens in the movies. My life has been almost like a movie since I got here. They say California makes magic and now I believe it.

Coming out of my bedroom I heard the house all a bustle. I walked into the living room and there were people cleaning and decorating. In the kitchen I found Michael. "Good morning, future Mrs. Stargate."

I stopped. *Oh my, that is going to be my name one day. This is just so weird.*

"Good morning future husband," I said, giving him a kiss. "Why are they doing this now? With these kids it will be a mess by noon," I said laughing.

"Well, I know you didn't want a maid but I figured you wouldn't mind one for a little while, at least until after the party. There will be someone here from six in the morning until midnight. After the party you can decide if you want to keep her or let her go," Michael said.

I was deep in thought. "I suppose that would be ok. Steph, grab a pen and paper so we can make a list and go to the grocery store. I need to start cooking pretty soon if I'm going to get this all done."

Michael looked at me strange. "Sweetheart you don't have to go anywhere," he laughed. "This is California, the home of movie stars. You just make your list and then we will have them deliver it."

Huh. I'm not so sure about all of this. "Michael, I appreciate that but I need to get it myself so I can make sure nothing is left out. I'm very anal about these things and it has to be done to my specifications. What am I supposed to serve at a Hollywood party anyway? I don't like caviar."

Michael walked over and puts his arms around me. "You have SO much to learn sweetheart. We don't just eat fancy stuff around here. Do you want to cook a meal or just appetizers?"

I hadn't really given much thought as to what we would eat at the party. With the way the week went I hadn't been able to give anything much thought. I really wanted to make a good impression on these people so one of them would take Constance and help her out. "What do you think we should do? You're her manager after all so this will reflect on you as well as me."

He thought about that a second and said, "Well I think both would be fine, if you can handle it all. We can set up the buffet on the bar and send trays around with snacks and appetizers. What do you think?"

If I can handle it all? He doesn't have a clue who he is talking to. I am used to cooking for an army so this will be a walk in the park.

"I think I can handle it and I think that sounds like a good idea. Now we just have to figure out a menu."

The three of us sat down at the table. "I think you should make a brisket, a pork roast like you do so well, and some kind of pasta," Steph said.

"Keep in mind sweetheart that some of these people are vegetarians. You need to make sure not everything has meat in it," Michael chimed in, "but other than that I think it sounds like a winner."

My mind was racing, "Okay, so here is what I think the menu should be, brisket, zesty Italian pork roast with angel hair, cheese lasagna for the vegetarians, potato salad, garlic toast, and for appetizers I will make crawfish dip on melba toast, crab and spinach dip on wheat crackers, mini pigs in a blanket, and for desert we will have a chocolate marble cake that I will make and decorate to commemorate the event. Is that enough?"

Michael astonishingly asked, "You can make all that?"

Steph laughed. "He hasn't been around long enough to know you and your kitchen has he? He'll figure it out."

Jonathan's parents and Steve came in for the weekend to help keep the kids occupied while we get everything done. They also wanted to be there for Constance's big day. If only I could enjoy some down time, but there is too much to do.

Monday morning Michael rolled over and kissed

me on the cheek, "Time to get up and get going. Today is the big day and you girls have a day at the spa to take advantage of."

I smiled and kissed him gently on the lips. "Thank you. You have been a ray of sunshine on a rainy day. I don't know what I would do without you."

He smiled. "Well, you will never have to find out sweetheart. I will always be here for you and those wonderful kids."

Jonathan's parents as well as the kids are downstairs when we make our way down and I can hear Constance going a mile a minute. Jonathan's mom, Mrs. Rosa, kissed me on the cheek and told me to have a good time. Michael chimed in, "Mrs. Rosa, I'm sorry, but you are going with them. It's all set up. You ladies go pick whatever you want and enjoy your spa day. It's all on me."

That brought a smile to her face. "Looks like you have a keeper here. You better be as good to him as you were Jonathan."

We headed to Rodeo Drive for dresses and then on to the spa. The day is amazing and relaxing, which is great because the night will be stressful even if everything goes as planned.

We arrived home and only have a couple of hours before the party. I went in the kitchen and gave directions to the staff, that Michael hired, as to how to handle the food. I walked in the living room and find Constance, Steph, and Mrs. Rosa were already dressed.

"Sweetheart you might want to get dressed. Mr. James will be here shortly so we can go over the last few details before everyone starts arriving." Michael said, rushing me out of the room.

In my room all I can do is stare at the beautiful gown I will be wearing tonight. It's a ten thousand dollar

Vera Wang, which I thought was unbelievably expensive. It was black sequined, straight fit that went all the way to the floor. The sleeves, if you want to call them that, were just off the shoulder spaghetti straps. The gown, the ring, the trip, it's all too much. I don't want to be spoiled like this. I like the simple things in life and if we are going to get married he is going to have to understand that. I put on the gown and look in the mirror. I felt and looked like a princess, considering I hadn't dressed up since I got here. The doorbell rang. It must be Mr. James. I grabbed my heels and headed down the hall.

I walked in the room and everything stopped. Everyone looked at me with their mouths on the ground.

Michael walked over. "You look amazing. Actually there are no words to describe how you look. I'm a lucky man."

He is showering me with compliments when Mr. James interrupted, "Wow Sherri! If your daughter grows up to look like you she will have every guy in the world knocking on her door."

I felt my face heating up and knew it was bright red. "I'm sorry Mr. James but Michael said something about last minute details."

Mr. James picked his jaw up off the floor, "Yes, I'm sorry. I'm just really shocked right now. Is there somewhere we can go and talk?"

Mr. James started explaining how things would work, "People will start getting here at least ten minutes late. They are never on time and have to make sure the paparazzi are here before they get here. I have already tipped off the paparazzi so it shouldn't be long before your front yard is a zoo. Don't worry; we will fix the damage after they leave. We didn't have all of them RSVP so it won't be a hundred people, but we still have a good shot. Once the guest list is all here we will get Constance on the stage to sing. She will sing at least four songs and by then we should have an offer. The money will go into a trust for her and once she finishes the tour she will get paid. Everyone here has a tour starting in the next two weeks so she will need to be ready to go. Any questions?"

I was dumbfounded. When I finally found my wits, "No I think that makes everything pretty clear. I have made a cake for the occasion so after she gets her offer we can bring out the cake if that's ok."

Mr. James laughed. "You have a strange way of doing things, but I like the way you think. We can turn it into a celebration party then."

I excused myself to go in the kitchen to make sure everything in there was going according to plan. The doorbell started ringing at ten after seven just like Mr. James said it would.

Since I am the hostess I'm going to be letting everyone in, I will not be letting a stranger do it. I opened the door and it was like everyone arrived at the same time. They each introduced themselves on their way in the door. First was Joseph, Nicholas and Kenny Johns, then Minny and Bobby Jones, James, Aaron, Kaden, and Leo of the band Those Boys, Sammy Groves, Macy Bosco, Demi Mitchell, Justin Knight, and Baylee Summers just to name a few. It was an "A" list of pop stars and their dates.

"We are only missing one and he said maybe so we can go ahead and get started. We should be able to find one out of this group that recognizes your daughter's talent," Mr. James told me before he took the stage. Once onstage he addressed the crowd, "Thank you everyone for making it. I believe the talent we have tonight will blow you away. Her name is Constance and she is a singer, songwriter, and dancer. I think you will be amazed. Let's not waste any more time. Constance will you come to the stage, please."

As Constance took the stage, the doorbell rings. I

opened the door and there stood Donovan Weston with his date, Amy Jones. "You aren't supposed to be here-" I started but before I could finish Mr. James was next to me.

"Welcome, Donovan. I'm so glad you can make it. Who is this pretty young woman?" Donovan introduced Amy to Mr. James as his friend.

Donovan pulled me to the side and explained, "I read the restraining order and it said I couldn't be here unless I was invited. Mr. James invited me but if you want me to leave I will understand. I'm really not here to start any trouble but let it be your decision not Michael's."

I opened my mouth but before I could speak Michael was by my side and grabbed my hand. "Look Donovan, the purpose of tonight is to help Constance so if you came here to start trouble you can leave now."

Donovan stuck his hand out to shake Michael's. "I personally have no intentions of starting any trouble. I'm here for the same reason as everyone else. We all want what's best for Constance, right?" Michael started to squeeze my hand. I could tell he wanted to rip Donovan apart but took Donovan's hand and shook it.

Constance took the stage with Michael and I close by for support. She starts to play and sing and everyone is amazed. After just one song Mr. James stops her.

"Constance, you don't have to play anymore if you don't want. We have found the star you will tour with."

Constance looked at him disappointed and asked, "But can I keep playing if I want?"

The crowd started to chant, "Let her play! Let her play!" Mr. James gave his consent and she continued to play.

Amy came over to Michael and I. Michael looks uncomfortable as he speaks to Amy, "Hey Amy," he said, "Sherri, this is Amy. Amy, this is my client's mother Sherri."

"It's nice to meet you, Amy. Please excuse me. I have to go get the cake."

His client's mother? Well it is a business party so maybe he is just trying to keep it professional. I won't let it bother me, my daughter is going to live her dream and it's all thanks to him.

Michael came into the kitchen, "I need to talk to you and it is really important-"

I cut him off, "Michael, I know what this is about and we can talk about it later. This is Constance's night and I want it to be all about her."

I walked out with the cake and Constance stopped playing and ran over. "WOO HOO CAKE!" Everybody laughed.

Mr. James took the stage again, "Everybody, Sherri has made a cake to celebrate the occasion. I know this is not how we normally do things but this child is not just another singer and I have never seen anything like what happened tonight. Everyone here made an offer and we ended up having a bidding war. The lucky singer is......Donovan Weston! Congratulations Constance. Now let's cut that cake."

Mr. James, Constance, Michael, myself, and Donovan stood behind the cake while everyone else sang 'For She's a Jolly Good Fellow'. Donovan put his arm around me and I turned and kissed Michael to show him he wasn't going to come between Michael and me.

The cake turned out to be a hit and everyone looked to be having a good time. Mr. James was talking to Donovan and Michael, getting things in order, and then walked off leaving Michael and Donovan alone. I'm curious of the conversation because it looks as if it's getting heated. This is Constance's night and I'm not going to let them ruin it. I'm going to put a stop to this once and for all!

I walked in between them looking Donovan in the

face, "Look, Michael and I are engaged to be married and he will be my daughter's manager. You have what you wanted, which is a piece of my daughter so the two of you can either get along or I can find someone else for her to tour with. Mr. James said everybody wanted to so I'm sure it won't be hard."

Donovan looked at me smiling, "You have a fire about you. I love that in a woman." I forgot where I was and what I'm doing and slapped him across the face. The entire room goes quiet.

"Did you not just hear me say Michael and I are engaged?" I shouted, not realizing I was doing so until the room was filled with silence.

Donovan was still holding his face when I heard the woman's voice from behind him. "So, you're engaged huh? And how did you think you were going to marry this tramp while we are still married? And what about your kids? You need to get your stuff out of my house NOW!" Amy said right before she slapped Michael.

Me, a tramp? Married? What the hell is going on?

I turned and looked at Michael, "You're already married?" I looked back and forth between Michael and Donovan and realized that everyone in the room had seen this whole scene. I ran to the kitchen, crying. I just wanted this to be Constance's night but now it had turned into a three- ring circus and it's all my fault.

Steph came in, obviously concerned, and asked, "What do you want me to do?"

I can't think. I don't know what to do. "Get rid of all these people please. I am so embarrassed I don't want to look at any of them." She turned to go out the door but stopped and asked, "What about Michael?"

I tried to gather myself. "I want Michael, Donovan, and Amy to stay. Everybody else should go. I don't want to ruin Constance's night, but I can't face these people after what just happened."

Steph hesitated, "What if we just move the party out of the house? I will make those three stay, but everybody else can move to the beach if they want."

"I guess that would be ok. I just don't want anyone in the house to see this. Ask Amy if she will please come speak to me. I can't blame her if she doesn't want to, but it's the only way I'm going to get clarity. Tell Donovan and Michael if they want any part of Constance's career they will stay right where they are until I'm ready to talk to them."

She came over and hugged me. "I will take care of it for you."

I stood in the kitchen trying to figure out how I got sucked into all of this when Amy walked in. "What do you want you husband-stealing tramp?"

She is upset and I can't blame her one bit but I have to plead my case and try to get some answers. "Look Amy, I'm so sorry about all of this. I know you think I'm stealing Michael but that couldn't be farther from the truth." Amy looked at me and you can see the hatred in her eyes. "I know you have no reason to believe anything that I have to say but if you will hear me out I think maybe you will understand a little better."

I told her all about Jonathan and what I was doing in California. I then told her I had absolutely no idea he was already married.

"You can't sit here and tell me you didn't know. It's all over the place. We have been married for years and have two kids together."

"Amy, trust me when I say I'm cut off from the world. I don't have much time for TV and I haven't been on the internet in years. I honestly did not know. He played the white knight to my damsel in distress and I fell for it hook, line, and sinker. I never had time to question his motives. Please, you have to believe me. I don't want to make enemies here."

Amy looked enraged. "Are you really that stupid? You have been here less than a week and already you are stealing husbands? Did you think that was going to make you friends?"

I'm trying to make her understand that I honestly had no idea when she lunged at me. She pulled my hair jerking my head back and reached for my hand. I broke free and tried to run for the living room but she threw a serving plate, which hit me in the head and knocked me to the floor. Before I could get back to my feet she jumped on top of me and we started struggling.

Steph came running in and grabbed her off of me. "STOP IT!! Y'all are acting like children over a man! He is NOT worth it."

Amy came at me again but Steph stepped between us.

The door opened. "Are y'all okay?" Michael asked.

"GET OUT!!" we both screamed. *At least we can agree on something.*

Steph continued, "Now look at the both of you. You are fighting like teenagers over a man who is CLEARLY not worth either of your time." She turned to Amy. "We have been cut off from the world since her husband was killed a year ago. She really had no idea."

I smiled and Amy shouted, "Of course you will take her side, you're her friend. How could you not?"

Steph looked at her and answered, "I'm not taking anyone's side. Everybody was duped by the guy." She turned to me, "And you Sherri. What can I say? You knew better than to get involved so seriously with someone you barely know. I have never known you to be so reckless."

Everybody was duped by the guy? What did Steph mean by that?

Amy and I looked at the floor as Steph continued, "Now if you want my opinion what I think needs to happen is y'all need to go out there together as a united front and confront the worthless piece of skin that calls himself a man, but in order to do that you are going to have to stop fighting amongst yourselves. Do you think you can be adult enough to do that? It's the only way you're both going to get the answers you deserve and want."

I looked at Amy and she looked at me. "I have no ill will towards you," I said to Amy. "Since my husband died I have lived like a recluse in my own little world. I'm so sorry and I never would have even talked to him had I known. He is a very good actor."

Amy looked at the floor for a minute and started to walk towards me. Steph stepped between us again. "I'm not going to play referee all night!"

Amy looked at her and promised, "I am not going to attack her again. Please let me by."

Steph looked at me as I asked, "Will you go get me some shorts and a shirt please. I can't play dress up anymore. It's just too exhausting."

As Steph headed out of the kitchen Amy apologized. "I'm sorry I attacked you," she said and smiled. "As bad as I hate to admit it, Steph is right. It's not you I should be mad at. We have the same enemy right now." She took my hand and looked at the ring. "And, you aren't going to believe this," she said showing me her ring, "but we have the exact same ring. He is really a piece of work. I should have known. If I promise not to attack you again can we put aside our differences just for tonight so we can get to the bottom of this?"

Genuinely smiling, I replied, "Yes I would like that. We both deserve the truth and the only way we will get it is to confront him together."

Steph came in with my clothes and updated us.

"The guys are asking what's going on. I hope its ok but I told them it was none of their damn business."

Amy and I both grinned. "That's perfect." Amy said.

As I changed clothes I felt as though I hadn't apologized enough to Amy. After all, she actually married the schmuck. "Amy I really am sorry. My family means everything to me and I would NEVER intentionally destroy another family. If anyone messes with my kids they will be sorry so I completely understand your anger."

We walked in the living room and for the first time since I have met the two of them Donovan and Michael stood in the same room without fighting. Michael walked over to me and took my hand, which I promptly snatched from him. "Don't touch me! If you EVER touch me again I can promise you will be sorry."

He looked at the floor. He can't even look me in the eye. "Sweetheart-" he started.

I lifted his head so he can look into my eyes and see that I was very serious. "Listen to me! Don't touch me and don't call me sweetheart. I don't want to hear anything out of your mouth but the truth."

Amy walked up next to me and told him, "We both want the truth. No, we don't want it, we deserve it."

He reached out to touch Amy and she slapped him. "Don't touch me either. We deserve answers and we will get them one way or another."

Michael pointed to the couch and asked, "Will you two please sit down?"

"No, we won't sit down. We want answers, NOW!" Amy demanded.

Donovan turned to Michael, obviously irritated, "Stop stalling and tell them the truth or I will!"

"You mind your business. This has nothing to do with you!" yelled Michael to Donovan.

Nothing to do with me? NOTHING to do with ME? I have let you use me and run over me long enough and it stops now. You tell them the truth or I will!" Donovan shouted.

Michael glared at him, "Seriously Donovan, SHUT UP NOW!" Michael yelled before turning back to us. "First, I'm sorry. I can't say that enough. Amy I was just trying to do what was best for our family."

Amy stopped him before he could lie anymore. "Do you really think that is going to work with me? I know you!"

I put my hand on Amy's shoulder to help calm her down. "Let him finish trying to run his lines on us."

Michael continued, "As I was saying, I was just trying to do what was best for our family. I never meant for anybody to get hurt." He turned to me, "Sherri, I'm sorry again. I got so wrapped up in what I was doing that I actually fell for you. I never lied when I told you I loved you."

Amy reared back and slapped him again. He looked at her and admitted, "I deserved that."

Oh, you deserve so much more than that sweetheart.
He still hasn't told us what he did.

"Michael," Donovan pushed, "Tell them. Tell them all of it now or I swear....."

Michael sat down and started his story, "It all started about six months ago. I ran across a video online of Sherri, Constance, and Drew playing and singing karaoke."

Amy looks at me questioningly, "You said you hadn't been on the internet. How did those videos get there?"

That's a very good question. I picked my jaw up off the floor and replied, "I swear to you Amy, I haven't been. I have no idea how they got there!"

Donovan interrupted, "Let him finish ladies. It will

all make sense in the end if he tells it all and tells the truth."

Michael cuts him a look that made me shiver, "Anyway," Michael continued, "I knew your daughter was going to be worth millions. I commented on the videos and left an email for the person that posted them to get in touch with me. It wasn't long before I got a response. I told them to get you and your daughter out here and I would make her a star. That person emailed me when you arrived and that's how I just happened to be on the beach that day. It was no coincidence. I wanted a piece of your daughter's career and I made it happen by becoming her manager. But Sherri you have to know once I met you, that all changed. The proposal was real. I really did fall for you."

Donovan, behind us, smirked and muttered, "I know she isn't that stupid."

I stood there dumbfounded about the video and just a little disgusted by Michael. "Who?" He looked at the floor so I screamed at him, "WHO? Who posted the videos and conspired with you?"

He stared at me for a few seconds but didn't answer my question. I lunged at him, wrapped both of my pretty little hands around his throat, and took him to the ground. I had him down on the floor strangling him when Donovan pulled me off.

Donovan wrapped his arms tightly around me trying to hold me in place. I screamed at him, "LET ME GO!"

Donovan leaned down and whispered in my ear, "Only if you promise to behave. If you don't get all the answers you want from him I will tell you. I promise."

He promises? I don't even know him and up until about five minutes ago I thought he was the bad guy.

"And why should I believe you?"

He smiled and replied, "Yeah, your right. You have no reason to believe me. But it's the truth."

I struggled with him and demanded, "Just let me

72

go!" He did reluctantly. Still wanting answers I turned back to Michael, "Are you going to answer me or am I going to have to hurt you?"

Michael started to speak but Steph walked in and started explaining, "It was me Sherri, but listen to me. Please don't hate me. I only wanted to help Constance. I never meant for you to accept his marriage proposal. I wanted to tell you but he threatened me once we got here that if I didn't keep my mouth shut he would make sure none of you were ever happy here and I can't stand the thought of that."

Well, shit.

She walked over to me, "Ever since Jonathan died, I just wanted y'all to be happy. I didn't realize I was dealing with a snake in the grass that would blackmail me. You will never know how sorry I am."

I hugged her. "It's okay Steph. I know you wanted the best for us and I can't fault you for that. It looks like we were all taken in by him. I am very upset that you didn't just tell me the truth."

I turned my rage on Michael, "You on the other hand! I will make sure you NEVER see a penny of my daughter's money." I took the ring off my finger and threw it at him. "You know what sucks about falling for a guy you know you're not right for? You fall anyway because you think he might be different."

Michael exploded. "You stupid bitch! I made your daughter's dreams come true. I'm the one that loves you and you forgive HER?" he screamed, pointing at Steph.

Donovan grabbed for Michael but before he could get to him Michael threw a punch that rocked my world and made me see stars, and I'm not talking about the Hollywood kind.

Chapter 6

Before I could do anything Donovan pinned Michael to the floor punched him over and over. I jumped up and grabbed Donovan trying to pull him off of Michael. "Killing him won't solve anything."

Donovan stood up and pulled Michael up, making sure he had a good hold on him. He turned to me and said, "Sherri I think you need to call the police."

Michael threatened, "And if you do I'm pressing charges on you and Donovan for assault."

I looked at Donovan and reluctantly said, "I can't make a bigger mess than this already is. Just let him go."

Donovan did as I asked and I addressed them all, "I want all of you out of my house now. If I ever see you again I will press charges."

Michael laughed while he wiped the blood from his lip, "You have to deal with me. You don't have a choice. I'm your daughter's manager and there is nothing you can do about it."

Donovan dragged him out by the arm. Amy, right behind them, paused and sincerely offered, "I'm so sorry, Sherri. I was all wrong about you. I'm so sorry you had to be on the receiving end of his rage. Again, I'm truly sorry." She turned and went out the door shutting it ever so slightly.

Steph put her hand on my shoulder, "I need to get back outside. I don't want to leave them outside by themselves for very long. Especially not after this fiasco."

I told her to go ahead and that I needed to be alone anyway. I went in the kitchen to get some ice from when Michael hit me.

How could I have been so stupid? I have to keep my head on straight around these people. They are good at

74

telling you what you want to hear to get what they want. Michael is right though. He is Constance's manager. I need to call the lawyer and see if there is anything I can do to terminate the contract.

I started walking to the back door, thinking what a big mistake I made by moving us to California. *How could I have thought that we would be okay out here? The worst part of all is that my mom was right. I'm so glad we don't speak so she can't say I told you so.*

I looked out on the beach and everybody was sitting around a bon fire singing and laughing. Constance is having the time of her life. *Maybe I did make the right decision. Anything worth having is worth fighting for. I should go out there, but I don't want anyone to see my face.* Constance saw me and I didn't have a choice. "Mom you HAVE to come out here."

I slowly walked out on the beach. One by one they all start coming up to me and telling me what a wonderful daughter I have. Nobody mentions my face, thank goodness.

"MOM! You're stealing my thunder!" Constance said. I laughed and went to find a seat. She came up to me and said "Mommy, watch this." She went in front of everyone and said "In the key of 'C' please."

I look around and several of the stars have gotten their guitars out. They all started playing and Constance started singing and dancing. She is still the star of the show and it was like the ordeal in the house never happened. What a relief to know it didn't dampen the party, for Constance's sake.

People started leaving and I knew the party was winding down and coming to an end. Constance had such a good time and I'm so proud of her. Now I just have to deal with all the drama her "manager" is going to dish out. The sun began peaking up. I didn't realize it was almost daylight. There are only about a dozen of us left when Joseph Johns got up and said, "Thanks for the party and sharing your daughter with us. We haven't had this much fun in a long time but we better get out of your hair."

They all agreed and got up to leave. Constance came running over, "But mom, don't let them leave without eating."

They all laughed and Joseph said, "I think everybody will agree when I say the only way we are staying to eat is if you get the same caterer from last night to do breakfast."

I blushed. "She is a little worn out but I'm sure she can whip something up for everyone."

Constance tugged on Joseph's shirt, "That wasn't a caterer silly, that was my mom. She is an awesome cook."

Jospeh looked at me stunned. "Is that true? That was some of the best food I have had in a while. You could go places out here if you put your name out there. I could help if you wanted."

Help me? I don't think so. I don't need any help from any more pop stars. I have been screwed over enough.

"Thanks, but I have to help my daughter right now, so I don't think I can." I said putting my hand on his shoulder.

He smiled at me. "Well if you change your mind, just let me know. I will be happy to help."

I smiled and tried to act like I was appreciative and muttered under my breath, "Yeah help. Y'all are good at that around here. More like destroying lives." Then headed into the house to get something together for breakfast.

With everyone full they finally decided to call it a night. On their way out they left me phone numbers and email addresses and told Constance to make sure she kept in touch. She was so excited that it didn't matter that she hadn't had any sleep.

I sent the kids to their room so I could get some down time. I really, really needed it. I haven't been alone since all this started. I tried to call the lawyer but he is out of the office until the end of the week so I left a message for him to call me back. Exhaustion took over and I fell asleep on the couch.

In my ear I heard, "Wake up sweetheart." I swung and slapped Michael only it wasn't Michael.

"Oh, I'm so sorry. Wait, what are you doing here? How did you get in here? I don't want any of you in my house! Get out!"

Donovan, still rubbing his face, commented, "That's quite a sting you have there. You could have handled yourself with Michael last night, huh?"

I tried to keep a straight face but smirked, "Yeah, I could have but I'm not that kind of woman. So, like I said I don't want you here. You need to leave."

He sat down instead and said, "I will leave but I needed to let you know that we will be leaving on tour in two weeks and you have a lot to do."

I got up from the couch hoping he would do the same, "I don't have anything to do. That's Michael's job as her manager. Now please leave."

He stood up, "Wow, you really want me to leave don't you?"

I looked at him in amazement. "What? You think because you're a big star I should just fall at your feet? I'm done with all of you except in a professional manner so there is no need to stop by or call or anything else for that matter. Everybody is getting what they wanted so just leave me alone and let me be her mother. It's all about the money with y'all and greed was never part of my plan."

He grabbed my hand. "Look, Michael-"

I stunned him when I snatched my hand back. "I

don't care about Michael. I don't care about you. I only care about my daughter and her well-being. NOW PLEASE LEAVE!"

As he headed for the door he replied, "I'm going to leave, but before I do a little piece of advice, Michael will never let Constance be happy."

I walked toward the door to close it behind him. "A little piece of advice for you as well," I said, "I wouldn't go around calling people sweetheart if you don't want to be slapped." and slammed the door.

The phone rang.

"Hello?"

"Hey sweetheart."

Jeez. It's Michael. I wanted to reach through the phone and slap him.

"Look, don't call me sweetheart anymore and you don't need to call here unless it concerns Constance. We have nothing more to say to each other unless it's about my daughter's career."

He sighed. "I am really very sorry."

I bet. I hung up the phone but before I could walk away it rang again.

"Hello?"

Michael hurriedly said, "Look if you're done being a bitch...."

I hung up again. The phone rang a third time but I refused to answer it. Steph came in and asked, "Do you want me to get that?"

"I don't care, but if it's anyone wanting to talk to me, I'm not home."

Steph answered the phone. A couple of minutes went by before she hung up.

"It was Michael. He said you need to have Constance at the stage tomorrow to start rehearsing with her new back up dancers."

I looked at her annoyed. I have two weeks I can kind of avoid these two, but after that I'm going to be stuck in a tour bus with them for months. I am not sure how I am going to handle it, but I have to for Constance's sake.

The phone rang again. I snatched it up and irritably said, "Look, I'm not dealing with any of this right now. If you want to talk about Constance that's fine, but I'm done listening to you otherwise."

The voice on the other end sounded shocked, "Sherri?"

I don't recognize his voice. "Yes, this is Sherri. Who is this?"

There was a long pause, "Sherri, this is Joseph Johns. Did I catch you at a bad time?"

I laughed, "No. I'm sorry Mr. Johns. Just dealing with California drama. What can I do for you?"

He laughed. "I'm so sorry you're having such a hard time out here. We aren't all like that. I feel bad that you got taken by the worst of us. But listen, that's not what I called about. I need a favor if you're willing."

Imagine that. A pop star that wants something from me.

"What can I do for you, Mr. Johns?"

He chuckled. "Please call me Joe. I'm not old enough to be Mr. Johns or even Joseph anymore. Look, what I need is…." I wait and nothing.

"Look Joe, I'm not being rude, but if you want Constance for something then it will have to wait because we leave to go on tour in a couple of weeks and she has a lot of work to do before we leave."

He finally spoke up, "No Sherri, actually I need you. I hate to even ask you, but you never know unless you ask right?"

Seriously? I know this kid is not going to ask me out. I'm done with anyone that works in the music or television industry. I can't date someone if I don't know when they are acting or when they are being themselves.

"Sherri?"

"Yes, I'm here."

He paused. "Look I'm going to cut right to the chase. I'm throwing a party next week and I was wondering, I mean I haven't, I mean….."

I cut him off, "Joe, just spit it out. You want Constance to sing? You will have to get in touch with Michael, but I think she has a lot on her plate already."

He said, "Ok before this gets anymore awkward, don't say anything and give me a minute to get my nerve up. I'm not calling for Constance. I wanted to know….. Wow, I never knew this would be so hard. I haven't found anyone who can cook like you…"- *Oh my! I was way off base. It's a good thing I didn't speak more of my mind or I would have been really embarrassed-* "and I know you said you didn't have time for a catering business but I was hoping maybe you would do this one party for me. You can bring the whole family."

I thought about it for a minute. "Well Joe, I'm not sure. Don't I need permits and all of that to do something like that?"

He answered, "Yeah, but I will take care of all of that. All you have to do is come to my house, use my kitchen, and cook the food. I will take care of everything else. And while you're here you and Constance can meet some of the GOOD people in the business."

Good people in the business? I'm pretty sure there aren't enough of them to make a party. I asked if I could think about it which he agreed and gave me his number to call him back with a decision.

The next morning we rolled out of bed and headed to the stage. I am so not looking forward to having to face Michael. Hopefully, we can keep this all professional but if

I know him that won't happen. I still haven't heard from my lawyer.

Constance ran onto the stage, "Mr. Michael, Mr. Michael, what are we doing today?" He turned to face her and you could see his whole attitude about her had changed.

He took Constance and introduced her to her back up dancers and choreographer. The rehearsal gets underway. I stood there and watched Constance thinking what a natural she is. She picked up the dance moves faster than the professionals. I'm so proud of her.

I am deep in thought when I felt a hand on my shoulder. "Sherri, can we talk?"

I shoved his hand off. "Michael, I have nothing to say to you unless it's about my daughter and I told you not to ever touch me again."

He got between the stage and me. "Sherri, we really need to talk about what happened."

I stared at him. "Are you really serious right now? There is nothing to talk about. It's done, we're done. We have a professional relationship and that is how it will stay. If that's a problem then I will make sure we never have to see each other again."

He grinned. "How are you going to do that? You can't stop me from being her manager, at least not for another year."

He thought he had me over a barrel. "No, but I can let Steph take over my duties and then I won't have to deal with you."

The smile vanished. "You wouldn't do that. Her career means everything to you and it would kill you to have to stay away and not see her succeed."

I looked him in the eyes. "Try me! Let me give you a little piece of information you might want to stick in your pocket and remind yourself every now and then. I'm not the weak, naïve woman you think I am. If you hadn't caught me at a vulnerable time, you would have NEVER gotten away with what you did. You might be able to fool and sweet talk your wife into believing your bull, but it stops here with me. I can be your worst enemy and I don't suggest you try it or you will find out the hard way."

I moved him from between the stage and me. "Now, was there something you needed to tell me about my daughter, or is this conversation done?" He turned and walked away pouting.

The remainder of the rehearsal went great. My baby is a natural but I never had any doubt.

"Tomorrow, Constance, we will work on singing and dancing at the same time." Michael said to her treating her like she was a moron that wasn't capable.

It irritated me immensely that he even has to have anything to do with her. I just want him out of our lives for good.

At home eating dinner the lawyer finally called me back. "Sherri, you called about your daughter's contract. Is that right?"

"Yes, I did. I wanted to know if there were any kind of loopholes in there that would let us out of the agreement." I explained.

"Well," he said, "Michael called and asked also and there is no way to get out of it unless you want to buy him out. And then if the buy-out is less than what her gross income is for a year then you will have to pay him the rest after the year is up."

A glimmer of hope. "And how much would that be?"

I can hear papers being shuffled, "Michael asked the same thing. I have the figures here somewhere. Give me just a sec."

He put me on hold. The longer I was on hold, the more nervous I got.

"Sherri, it's going to come to about two hundred fifty thousand."

I almost fainted. "DOLLARS?!?" I squeaked.

He laughed, "Well, yes. If things go the way they are slated to, she will make one point five million this year alone."

Numbness spread over me. "Okay, thank you. If I decide to I will call you back."

I hung up the phone and wobbled over to the table with my mouth still on the floor.

"What did he say, Sherri?" Steph inquired.

I looked at her speechless for a couple of seconds. "He said…that they think…" I am barely able to get the words out, "they think…they think Constance will make about one and a half million dollars just this year."

Steph's mouth hit the ground. "Oh my god! That's crazy money. What did they say about Michael?"

"Well he gets fifteen percent of her gross income, so if I want to get rid of him as her manager it's going to cost me two hundred fifty thousand dollars."

Steph sat there stunned. "So what are you going to do?"

I looked at her and shook my head. "There isn't much I can do. I don't have that kind of money right now, and by the time she makes that much his contract will be up. So, I guess I will just have to deal with it.

"Are you going to be able to do that?" Steph asked.

"I don't know but I have to try for Constance's sake. I can't just keep her from her dream because I screwed up."

The next morning we sat at the studio for Constance to practice her dancing and singing. I never knew so much went into getting a show together. I felt a hand on my shoulder and jump about three feet in the air. My first thought was to knock Michael on his ass so he would stop putting his hands on me.

"You people LOVE to sneak up on folks, don't you?" I said looking at Donovan. "Unless you want to talk about Constance there is nothing for us to talk about. What are you even doing here?"

He swept the hair out of my face and looked at the stage, "She is a natural isn't she?"

I looked at Constance having so much fun. "Yeah, they say she will make over a million this year." I looked back at him. "That was none of your business. I really don't have to talk to you. It will be bad enough being stuck with you and him on the tour bus for months at a time. Just leave me alone. Unless you have something that concerns Constance, I really don't want to talk to you."

He turned to leave but hesitated. "I know you don't want to talk to me, but Michael-"

I cut him off, "I really don't care about the drama between you and Michael. I don't want to hear about it and I'm not going to let it affect my daughter. We all have to be stuck together for a while so why don't we all agree not to talk to each other and the two of you need to try to get along. I will NOT let my daughter get dragged in the middle of all this. It has nothing to do with her."

"I can understand but eventually you will have to listen to me. You will want to hear what I have to say. I'm not taking up for Michael, but it does concern Constance, and you for that matter."

Before I could say anything he stormed out of the studio.

On the ride home, Constance is going a hundred miles an hour like she has since we started this whole thing.

"Mom," she began, "I was wondering if you would get on stage with me."

"Constance, I can't be up there with you. This is for you. I can't do it for you and as much as I want to be up there with you, they won't let me."

She is disgusted, "NO mom, I get to sing with Donovan and I want you to be up there with us. You can do it. I know you can. Please mom?"

I told her I will think about it.

The next day I got out of bed and relaxed a little remembering that we don't have to go to the stage or studio today and could take a little break. All the excitement is about to take its toll on me. We have to work on packing today because we don't know when we will have time to again.

I went in the kitchen and am full of energy so I decided we will have a big breakfast. I heard the doorbell and went to see what early morning visitor came to see us. I opened the door and saw Donovan, "Ughh… you people just don't give up, do you?"

He laughed, "I'm here to work on the song Constance and I are going to write and sing together. I promise to stay out of your way and leave you alone."

Constance came running, "Donovan! I'm so happy to see you. Mom said she would think about singing and dancing with us."

He picked her up. "That's so awesome. I'm sure your mom will do just as well as you do if she joins us." He turned to me, "Where did you want us to work on this?"

I pointed to the kitchen. "Constance you can work till breakfast is done and then you have to take a break, deal?"

"Ok mom. Is that okay Donovan?"

He smiled at her, "It sure is sweet pea. Let's get

started."

They sat at the table and start working while I cooked breakfast.

"Ok," I said, "Lets clean off the table so we can eat and then y'all can start again." I turn to Donovan. I'm not going to be rude even though I don't want him in my house. "Would you like to eat?"

Donovan smiled genuinely, "If it's your cooking I wouldn't pass that up for the world." My body betrayed me and I blushed before I realize what I was doing.

Chapter 7

Sitting at the table Donovan asked Constance, "So, Constance, what do you think of Michael as your manager?"

I shot him a dirty look. "Donovan that is not a question you need to ask her." Constance ignored me and answered the question, "He's mean. I thought I would like it but he gets onto me if I mess up just one time. It's like he expects me to be perfect all the time. I don't like working with him."

Shocked, I asked, "Constance, why haven't you told me this?"

She gazed at me. "Well, I want to do this and he has to help me or else I can't sing and dance."

I put my hand on her shoulder. "Baby, that isn't true. You can sing and dance without him."

She started crying. "No, I can't mom. He told me without him I would never be allowed to sing or dance." She jumped up and ran out of the room.

I looked angrily at Donovan. "Do you see what you did? Why should I let you work with my daughter anymore? I think you need to leave."

"What I did? I just thought you needed to know the truth and you would have ignored it coming from me." He stood up. "Sherri, can't you see what he is doing? You are blaming it all on me. When are you going to wake up and realize he is bad news?"

I started to cry and screamed at him, "What am I supposed to do? I just want to protect my daughter. I talked to my lawyer and I can't stop him."

He came over and put his arms around me. "Sherri, he can be stopped. I promise I can take care of it for you."

I jerked away from him and replied, "And THEN I

would be in YOUR debt. Nobody does anything out here just to be nice. They have to get something out of it or they don't do it. I don't need help from any of you! Just get out of my house!"

He turned to leave. "Tell Constance we will work on the song later when everybody has calmed down. And, just so you know, I can fix this for you but you have to want it. I'll be back later." He stormed out of the house and slammed the door and I went to check on Constance.

At lunchtime Donovan showed back up. "Let's just forget about the conversation earlier. I don't want to make things harder on Constance. I just want y'all to be happy," he said.

I chuckled remembering how Michael wanted nothing but our happiness. "Yeah, I've heard that before."

I told them they could work in the kitchen while I got lunch ready. "Looks like I made it right in time, " he said, smiling. "I really enjoy your cooking. I hope I'm not imposing."

I don't want to be rude. "No, it's no imposition."

It took a couple hours but they finally finished their song. "Constance, you have real talent. I have never written a song so fast. We need to test it out. What do you think?" Donovan asked Constance.

She smiled at me. "Mom will you listen to it, please?"

We went into living room where they performed the song. The song is absolutely amazing. I'm so proud of her. I hugged her and told her, "Your daddy would have been so proud of you. You're quite the young lady."

Donovan looked puzzled. "Not to but in but what happened?"

Constance looked at him upset and said, "My daddy blew up."

I put my hands on her shoulders and explained, "He

88

was killed in an accident almost a year ago. I would rather not talk about it. I have poured my heart out to enough stars since I got here."

He leaned down and put his arms around her. "I'm so sorry sweet pea. Let's not talk about that right now."

Constance broke away from my grip. "Do you have to go now or can you stay for a little while?"

He looked at me. I got a disgusted look on my face. "I guess its okay as long as you can keep your mouth shut."

He grabbed her hand. "Hey, why don't we grab your brothers and go out on the beach and throw a Frisbee? It will be a long time before we have time to do that again once we hit the road." Hand in hand they walked out to find the boys.

On our way to the stage the next morning I decided I was going to put my foot in Michael's ass for treating my daughter the way he had. There is no way I will let him ruin what could be the best time of her life. He is waiting when we walked on the stage.

"Constance, go get dressed and warmed up. I need to talk to Michael," I told her and she walked off.

"So, you're ready to talk now? I knew you would come around," he said smiling.

All I wanted to do was slap him. He is so arrogant and full of himself it makes my skin crawl just to have to talk to him.

"No, you conceited jerk! It's about Constance. You're being entirely too hard on her. This is supposed to be fun and she is miserable. She is a child and is going to make mistakes. Don't make this so hard for her."

He smiled his evil smile. "That's the business. If she can't hang maybe she shouldn't be doing this. She can go find a playground to play on. While she works for me she will do as I tell her and there is nothing you can say or do

89

about it. I know you tried to buy me out of my contract but I also know you don't have enough money to do that so you're stuck. Either deal with me and make her dreams come true or ditch me and your daughter will hate you for holding her back. The choice is yours."

I spent the rest of the day avoiding him but trying to keep my daughter safe. She cried all the way home because of how Michael treated her.

"Constance, do you want to stop all of this?" I asked.

Crying, she answered, "Mom, I really love it and want to do it but Michael is SO mean. Can't we just get away from him?"

I wished I could help her but we don't have that kind of money. What else is there I can do? After the way he talked to me and the way he is treating Constance I swear he is only doing this to get back at me. *GOD, I just want to strangle him.* I smiled as I thought about strangling him.

"Mom, what is so funny?"

I stopped smiling. "I'm sorry honey. I will see what I can do about it. Just try to do what he tells you until I can get this taken care of."

At home I told Steph about the gall Michael had and how he is treating Constance.

"Sherri, Donovan offered to help didn't he?" she asked.

"Yeah, he did but what's that going to cost me, Steph? I mean I have already been sucked in by one star. Do I really need to go there again?"

Steph looked me over a few seconds before responding. "Sherri, what is it costing you now? Is it really worth it? He said he could make your daughter happy. What's the harm in hearing him out?"

I know she is right even though I hate to admit it. I'm very skeptical but I guess hearing him out wouldn't hurt anything. I hesitantly picked up the phone. I dialed all of

the numbers but the last before I hung up. *Come on Sherri,
you can do this. Your daughter's career and welfare are at
stake.* I dialed the number before I could think twice.

"Hello?" he answered. Silence. "Hello?" he said again.
I couldn't find the courage to make myself speak. About
that time Constance came running in the room. I covered
the receiver and whispered to her, "Constance, its
Donovan. Ask him to come over for dinner."

She grabbed the phone and had no trouble with her
courage. "Hey Donovan, its Constance. My mom wanted
me to ask you to come over for dinner."

I didn't mean for her to make it sound like my idea,
even if it was. She is quiet for a moment and then said,
"Sure. Hold on," and handed me the phone.

"Hello?" I said quietly.

"Sherri, do you really want me to come over for
dinner? I have already told you I love your cooking so
don't play with me."

I took a deep breath before I spoke. "Okay Donovan,
there is something I need to talk to you about in person.
The only way I will let you come over here is if you answer
only the questions I ask and don't try to get me involved in
the drama between you and Michael. I have had enough
drama to last me a lifetime."

He hesitated momentarily. "Okay, so is that an
invitation?" he asked, laughing.

"Yes, please join us for dinner on those conditions."

"I'll be there," he said.

Sitting at the table I made small talk. I didn't want to
discuss everything in front of the children. When we were
finished eating I asked Steph to put them to bed.

"Can I do it, please?" Donovan asked.

I am shocked and very hesitant. The last person that
was this nice used my kids to get into my life and heart and

91

I just can't let that happen again. I hesitantly agreed.

"I will get us something to drink meet you in the living room," I told him.

When he came into the living room I was sitting in a chair. I don't want to be any closer to him than I had to. He took a seat on the couch.

"I don't really know where to start, Donovan," I began and he moved to the end of the couch closer to me.

"Take your time and breathe slowly. You can do this," he said smiling.

"You're really enjoying this, aren't you?" I asked.

"Not really," he said, "I hate to see anyone so unhappy. It bothers me that Michael…I'm sorry. I almost forgot the rules. Go ahead. What did you need to talk to me about?"

I looked at the floor. "You said you could help me. I want to know how and what it's going to cost me."

He leaned over and lifted my face so that I was looking in his eyes. "Sherri, I know it was hard for you to come to me, especially after all you have been through. I also know it must be really bad for you to turn to me so I'll make it easy for you. I can get Michael's contract voided for you. Have you talked to your lawyer?"

I started crying. "I have. He told me there was no way other than buying Michael out and there is no way I can do that."

He leaned over and wiped the tears from my cheek. "Then we will talk to another lawyer. The lawyer you're using is also Michael's lawyer and he has no loyalty to you so he isn't going to try to help you in any way. I will handle it all and I will make sure it's taken care of. I will need you to sign the papers, of course."

I dried my eyes. "Yes, of course, but before I agree to this what is it going to cost me? Nobody does anything in this town without wanting something and I can't get into another situation like before."

An evil grin spread over his face. "It will cost you dinner with me."

I stammered, "So, all I have to do is cook you dinner and we are even? I don't believe you."

"No," he said, "I said it would cost you dinner with me. You won't be the one cooking. I want to take you to dinner."

Here we go again. What is it with these people?

"Donovan, I have already told you I want nothing but a professional relationship yet you are still hitting on me. I want my daughter to be happy but I just really don't think I can put myself back in that position."

He smiled. "Fine then. It can be a professional dinner. Just agree to dinner, will you? "

"Donovan, that sounds good but I have learned there is always an underlying motive behind things of this size. I tell you what, I will agree to dinner but nothing more and we are NOT flying anywhere to do it. I don't even know when we will have time. I have that dinner to cook for next week and then we leave for the tour."

He smiled and tried to assure me, "Just let me worry about that. Do we have a deal?" He could obviously see the worry in my eyes. "I promise you, dinner is all it will be."

"I guess dinner would be okay but if you do anything out of line then I'm done and the deal is no longer good."

He laughed. "I can live with that. Let me step outside and call my lawyer. He is going to want to know whom you want as her manager. What should I tell him?"

I don't have to think twice about my answer. "Me," I said, "I will handle her career, and if I have any problems I will work it out from there."

He took my hand. "Sherri, I think that's a great idea. I know you can handle it. I have faith in you. I will be right back," he said and then stepped outside.

I can't help but wonder if I have done the right thing. *Stop second-guessing yourself. Your daughter deserves to be happy doing what she wants to do. Michael is going to be mad, but he brought it on himself. You don't threaten me or my family and think you're going to get away with it.*

Donovan walked back in and announced, "It's all taken care of."

My jaw dropped to the floor. "How did you do that? You're joking, right? You're just saying this to get me out to dinner."

He wrapped his hands around my face. "I wouldn't do that and we won't have dinner until it's all settled, just so you will know I'm not lying. My lawyer is going to file an injunction tomorrow. It will take a couple of days and may take a little while to finalize but by the time we leave to go on tour he will no longer be her manager."

So elated and excited about everything, I forgot what I was doing and hugged him. I quickly pulled away. "I'm sorry. I never thought I would be so relieved."

He smiled, "Oh, it's perfectly alright. I don't mind. We need to keep this quiet until he is served the papers though. If not he will make Constance's life a living hell. I will tell him tomorrow that she and I need to work on our song so that I can keep an eye on him until this is all resolved."

I look at him puzzled, "And what is that going to cost me?"

He grinned. "How about one more home-cooked meal and we will call it even?"

I thought carefully before I replied, "I suppose I can do that. But again, no funny stuff."

He left and for the first time in a year I got on the Internet. I'm going to make sure I'm not stepping on anyone's toes this time. It's only dinner but I don't want to have dinner with a married man or even one that has a girlfriend. It's been so long since I have been on the

Internet that I forgot how informative it was. I found out he is newly single and seems to be a stand-up guy. But, of course, that's what they are supposed to look like to the public. I will keep my guard up this time for sure. I decided I better research what I'm supposed to be doing as Constance's manager.

I am still up when the sun came up. I decided I shouldn't say anything to Constance about Michael so that she doesn't tip him off.

At the stage call Donovan kept his word and is there to rehearse with her and keep Michael in check.

Michael walked over to me. "So, I hear you had dinner with Donovan last night. I guess he told you all kinds of lies about me. So, you're dating him now?"

I snapped at him, "Donovan and I had a business dinner last night. We are not dating, but even if we were it's none of your business."

Michael laughed. "Well, he is a snake in the grass so I wouldn't be alone with him. He isn't the gentleman I am," he said and walked off.

This feud between them is really starting to get under my skin. What kind of lies is he so worried about Donovan telling me? Why does it matter what I'm doing? It's none of his business. The only thing he needs to worry about is my daughter until I take that away from him too.

Shouting interrupted my thoughts and I looked up to see that Michael had stormed the stage and was in Donovan's face.

"So, you're taking my sloppy seconds again?" Michael shouted.

"Sloppy seconds? I don't know what you're talking about but you know I never take anything from you. It's the other way around, don't you think? You tried to take everything from me!" Donovan shouted back.

"You can have the slut! She isn't worth the trouble. I have what I wanted, which is part of her daughter," Michael yelled.

Donovan punched him and I ran and grabbed Constance, who was stuck in the middle of this. "STOP IT, BOTH OF YOU!! Y'all should be ashamed of yourselves!"

I took Constance and we left. I don't ever want to see either one of them again although the more I think about what was said the more I wonder what is really going on between these two. Regardless, I don't want to look at either one of them to ask.

We walked in the house and Steph was waiting on us. "Both of them called. What happened today? They tried to say they needed to talk about Constance but I got the feeling they were lying."

"Yes, they were."

We sat down and I told her about what happened.

"What was all that about sloppy seconds and Donovan saying Michael took everything from him?" Steph asked.

"I don't know and I don't want to know. I just know I don't want Constance around either of them until all of this is settled."

I woke up to my phone going off. I checked it and it was a text from Donovan. Constance must have given him my cell phone number. Do I even want to read it? With everything going on I'm just physically, mentally, and emotionally drained. I wanted to ignore it but it could be important.

I washed my face, sat on my bed, and picked up the phone trying to convince myself to read it. I finally gave in and read the message. *Injunction in place. Meet me @ lawyers office to sign the paperwork @ 9.* It went on to give the address.

I glanced at the clock and realized I didn't have long to get ready.

"Steph," I hollered, "Can you watch the kids today? I have to go take care of some legal stuff."

She stuck her head in my door. "Yeah, no problem. What's going on?"

"I just have to go meet Donovan to take care of the Michael situation."

A look spread across her face, one of those *I told you so* looks. "I told you he could take care of it. Good luck," she said as she left me to get ready.

Chapter 8

I made it to the office just in time. Donovan was waiting and met me at the car. "Hey. I was worried you wouldn't read the message. I'm so sorry about yesterday –"

I stopped him, "I really don't want to talk about yesterday. I'm on the verge of a nervous breakdown because of the two of you and it's not fair to my daughter or to me. Let's just get this done and then I can deal with the rest of it."

He contemplated that for a moment and said, "Okay. I'm sorry I keep pushing. Mr. Johnson is waiting on us."

As we walked into the office Donovan made the introductions.

"So, this is Michael's newest victim," Mr. Johnson stated more than asked.

I looked back and forth between them. "What do you mean by that?"

Mr. Johnson put papers in front of me. "Well, let's take care of business and then if you want me to explain I can but Donovan would be the better person to fill you in." I signed the papers. Why did it feel like I was signing my life away again? "Okay, Sherri. That's it. You are no longer a part of Michael's scam. You're lucky you came across Donovan or you would have been miserable for the next year. Michael isn't going to take this very well. Do you want to go ahead and sign a restraining order while you're here just to be safe?"

Victim? Scam? What the hell is going on? I won't leave this office without some answers, that's for sure.

"Yes, let's do please. I can't deal with any more drama. I have had enough."

Mr. Johnson laughed. "Yeah, that sounds like Michael. It will take me a few minutes to draw up the papers. Why don't you and Donovan go get a coffee next door or something and by the time you get back I will be ready for you to sign them."

We walked out of Mr. Johnson's office and out of the building where we continued on in silence. I don't know how to go about asking him and he isn't going to volunteer anything because I have told him too many times I didn't want to hear it.

We got to the coffee shop and stood in line to be waited on. I tried nonchalantly to start the conversation figuring if I opened the door he would walk through it. "So," I said staring at the menu, "I really appreciate this and I know Constance does too."

He didn't look at me either. "Sure thing. I couldn't stand the thought of knowing that y'all were miserable and I had the power to fix it for you. It should have never happened to begin with. I know Michael..." he stopped and quickly added, "Sorry. I didn't mean to bring that up."

Well that didn't go as I had planned. He was finally listening to me and not talking about the Michael drama. The difference was now I WANTED to know about the Michael drama. He was going to make me ask.

"It's okay," I said, "I actually want to know. Now that he isn't a part of mine or Constance's lives anymore I think I'm ready."

We got our coffee. "Let's sit here a few minutes and talk. Mr. Johnson will be waiting on us when we get back," he said. We sat down and he continued, "I have been trying to tell you this since you got here –"

Before he could say anything else three little girls came running over to the table. "Mr. Donovan, can we have your autograph?" the oldest one asked, blushing.

He smiled at them. I watched him as he dealt with these kids and it seems he really has a soft spot for children but it could be an act after all.

When we were alone again he turned back to me.
"Sorry about that. I just can't say no to a fan, especially not
a child. Like I was saying, I have been trying to tell you
this since you got here but Michael made it almost
impossible. The story he gave you was only half true –"

I interrupted, "Which story?"

He looked puzzled and said, "The one at the party.
Which other one was there?"

I told him about the conversation in the limo where
Michael explained the drama between them. He was
obviously angry. "I should have known. That story is a lie.
I swear sometimes he convinces himself that his lies are
true. Okay, well, I will tell you the whole story. You can
believe me or not but if you ask anyone else you will see
that I'm actually telling the truth and that anything you
heard from Michael was a lie."

He hesitated, took a deep breath, and continued, "It all
started with the video. Michael did see it but only because I
was watching it and he happened to see it over my
shoulder. I did email Stephanie, but I did NOT email her
about Constance. I emailed her about YOU."

I looked at him crazy. "Me? Why me?"

He stopped me, "Let me finish telling you this before I
lose the chance yet again. Anyway, she never emailed me
back. I heard through the grapevine that Michael had
contacted her and that y'all were moving out here. There is
always some kind of gossip going around this town so I
tend not to believe anything until I know it to be fact. When
I ran into y'all at the studio I knew what had happened. I
warned him, but he swore he was done being a jerk and this
was for real. I told him I would be watching him. When I
figured out his motives weren't pure is when I started
trying to warn you, but he made it hard for me to get to
you, and you made it even harder to tell you the truth."

I started to apologize. "I'm so sorry, but how did you

know what he was up to?"

He smiled at me. "I won't hold it against you. You're new to this town and had no idea. You were just doing what you thought was right. I know all about Michael because he did the same thing to me. He almost ruined my career before I even got started. If I hadn't found Mr. Johnson I wouldn't be the person I am today. I hated being treated that way and almost quit. As for Amy, she and I was never an item. There was a rumor going around that we were dating so he decided to try to 'take her away' from me. He didn't have a hard time because she was never mine, but he has been after my career ever since he claims I double-crossed him. Trust me when I tell you this isn't over with him, but you are on the right track, and if you can handle him then your daughter will be very successful. I will be there to help if that's what you want, but I have figured out you're a very strong woman that doesn't like to let other people fight her battles so if you want me to back off I can do that too. You just tell me what you want and I will do it."

I started crying. "How could I have been so stupid? Why didn't I see right through him? Before Jonathan's death my bullshit monitor would have blown him out of the water."

He got up from his seat, walked to me, and lifted me up into his arms. "I'm so sorry. I did all I could to try to help but you wouldn't let me and I wasn't going to force you."

I just collapsed into his arms. "But why did you want me? I don't have half the talent my daughter does. Did you just want me so you could get to her? I don't understand."

He pulled me away, lifted my head, and dried my tears. "Trust me when I say it had nothing to do with your daughter but I can't tell you right now why I wanted you. It was nothing bad but you have been through enough and if I told you why right now you wouldn't believe me.

Eventually you will figure everything out. Now let's get back and sign those papers so we can get out of here. You have a party to start cooking for and Constance and I have a song to practice."

On our way back to Mr. Johnson's office I tried to work up the courage to ask him for a favor. He has already done so much for us and I don't want to ask for more, but I don't think I can do this on my own. "Donovan," I said, "Do you think you could go with me to tell Michael? I want to be the one to tell him face to face. I'm not a coward and I'm not going to hide behind lawyers."

Donovan stopped and looked at me. "Yes I will be glad to, but if he starts on you…"

I smiled. "Oh trust me; if he starts on me he will be very sorry."

Donovan stops, "Oh, I do trust you and I have seen how very sorry he will be."

With everything signed and filed it is time to go break the news to Michael. Donovan started to get in his car and asked, "Do you want to drop your car off at your house, and we can just take mine?"

I don't see anything wrong with it so I agree. "I would like to take Constance also. She should be there so that she knows what's going on."

He looked at me questioningly, "Are you sure that's a good idea? You know how explosive his temper is and if he lays a finger on either of you, you're not going to be able to stop me from killing him this time."

"Yeah, it will be fine. She deserves the satisfaction of being able to tell him off if she so pleases. I don't normally condone it, but after what he has put her through I'm not going to make her mind her manners."

We dropped off my car and picked up Constance. I explained to her what we were going to do and told her that she was welcome to say something to him if she felt the need. Michael is at the stage when we arrive.

I walked straight up to him with Constance right behind me. "Michael, I guess you know why we are here."

By the looks of it he is pretty angry. "Yeah, I heard what you did with the help of your new boyfriend. You think you're smart, don't you? First you fell for my lines and now you're falling for his. Let me guess, he is her new manager?" He turned to Donovan and continued, "I bet you're proud of yourself, finally getting one over on me, huh?"

I stepped in front of him. "Not that you deserve any explanation but he is NOT my boyfriend, I am NOT falling for any lines, and I know the truth. I know what you did to him and were trying to do to us. He is NOT her manager, I am."

Michael started to laugh hysterically. "You? Her manager? You won't last a day out here. I wasn't lying about the sharks and you are fresh meat. You will come crawling back, watch."

Constance stepped in front of me. "You know my mom always taught me to be a nice girl, but you're a jerk! There is no way I will ever work for you again. I'll quit first. I was wrong to have EVER thought you were a good person. I will tell everybody I see what kind of a person you REALLY are!"

Michael slapped her. I stepped up to punch him but Donovan beat me to it. He knocked Michael out cold. I turned to Donovan, "Call the police. I'm done with this. I am pressing charges against him."

The police showed up and took statements from everyone. Once they had everyone's statements they handcuffed Michael and as they led him out one officer came over and addressed Donovan, "Sir, I need you to put your hands behind your back. You are being placed under arrest for assault."

I freaked out. "But officer, he was just defending my child. You can't be serious."

The officer replied, "Unfortunately ma'am, I am. Mr. Stargate wants charges pressed so I have no choice."

Donovan is very calm about the whole thing. "Sherri, listen to me carefully. Call Mr. Johnson and tell him what happened. He has the money to come get me out of jail. I will call you when I get out. Just be strong. It will all be okay."

I called Mr. Johnson as they took Donovan out. He said he would take care of everything. As I am leaving the stage my cell phone rang. I fished it out of my purse and saw that it was Steph calling. I answered, "Hey Steph! I can't talk right now. I have to get to the police station."

She said, "I know. I was wondering if you wanted me to meet you there and get Constance. You don't need to deal with her while you're dealing with all of this right now."

"Yes, please. I will meet you there."

I hung up the phone and headed to the police station. My mind slowed down and I started thinking. Steph said she knew when I said I was going to the police station. How did she know? It doesn't matter. I don't have time to worry about that right now. I have to get there in case Mr. Johnson gets held up. I will not let him sit in jail. This is all my fault.

We made it to the police station a few minutes before Steph but I was so relieved when she got there. "Thank you so much Steph. She doesn't need to be around all of this but how did you know what was going on?" I asked.

"You wouldn't believe it, but someone that was there took video of it and it's all over you tube. It's the top watched video. I can't believe he hit Constance," she replied.

I just stared at her in amazement. "Are you serious? That's all I need is for everyone to know my business."

Steph smiles. "Well, I bet after watching it they don't mess with you."

Steph and Constance were leaving as Mr. Johnson pulled up. "Sherri, I will be right back. This shouldn't take long. You wait here."

I waited for what seemed like an eternity. When Donovan and Mr. Johnson finally came out I ran over to them, put my arms around Donovan, and started apologizing profusely. "I'm so sorry. I'm so sorry. This is all my fault."

He stood there shocked. Mr. Johnson told him, "I will contact you later. Just remember what I said."

I backed up and looked into Donovan's eyes. "He told you to stay away from me, didn't he?" I asked, dreading his answer.

Donovan smiled. "No babe, he wants me to stay clear of Michael and stay out of trouble until after the trial."

My mouth dropped open. "Trial? Oh no, what have I gotten you into?"

He laughed. "You haven't gotten me into anything and you worry too much. What are you doing here anyway? I told you I would call you."

I was on the verge of tears. "I have your car and I didn't want to leave you stranded."

He took my hand. "I would have gotten a ride to your house to get my car. You have another reason for being here, don't you? You like me a little bit, huh?" he asked, an adorable smirk on his face.

I snatched my hand away blushing, "No, I was just worried you wouldn't have a ride. So, what is this about a trial? What's going on?"

He took the keys from me. "We'll talk about it on our way to your house. Let's go before the paparazzi get here please. I have had enough excitement for one day." We laughed and headed for the car.

The kids were so excited to see both of us as we walked into the house. After a few minutes of playing with Donovan I convinced them to go play by inviting him for dinner.

Steph was in the kitchen helping me when Donovan came in. "I will tell you what happened but you have to promise not to freak out."

Steph laughed and replied, "Her freak out? Are you serious?"

I gave her a dirty look then turned to Donovan and said, "I promise."

He sat at the bar. "Well, Michael is mad because you pressed charges on him so he figures if you're going to send him to jail that I am going with him. Anything to keep me away from you is his goal. Basically, we will both go to trial, not together of course. A jury will decide our guilt or innocence so I really don't think there is anything to worry about."

I tried to interrupt but he stopped me. "This is not your fault. It's Michaels. I would have never stood by and watched him lay a finger on you or your daughter, or anyone else in this family for that matter. I have had enough of him and it's time he got what's coming to him. Stop blaming yourself. It will all be okay."

"But what about the tour? How will you still go on tour if you have to be here for court?"

He smiled. "This is where I'm going to sound like an arrogant ass, which I hate doing, but I have money, babe. I will hop a flight back from wherever we are and come to court."

I walked over and put my hand on his. "I will be coming with you. You can say what you want but this is partly my fault and I'm going to be there to testify on your behalf."

He grabbed my hand, "Anything you say, babe."

I pulled my hand back. *What is with the babe stuff? He probably calls everybody that. Stop over analyzing stuff and over reacting.*

Once dinner was over and the kids were in bed Donovan grabbed his coat. "I suppose I better get going."

I found myself wanting him to stay but after all the trouble I have caused him I'm not going to ask. "Yeah, I guess. What is on the agenda for tomorrow?"

He stopped and thought about my question for a moment. "Well, since we got nothing done today we need to get working on that song, Constance and I do anyway. You need to get started on the menu for that party. It's coming up pretty quick."

I stared off into space. "Yeah, I guess you're right. Do you want to work on the song here where I can work on the party stuff?"

He kissed me on the cheek. "Sounds good to me. I will see you tomorrow."

He opened the door to walk out as my phone rang. He turned around and asked, "You expecting a call?"

I shook my head no and answered the phone. "Hello?"

I knew the voice in an instant. I tried hiding it so that Donovan wouldn't know who it is.

"I'm going to talk and you're going to listen because I hold all the cards," Michael said. "You have two choices here. You can either drop the charges and have the paperwork changed to make me Constance's manager again or you can let your little boyfriend serve two to ten for assault. The choice is yours sweetheart. Call me when you make a decision."

He hung up and I stood there with the phone in my

hand, stunned. Donovan, standing at the door, asked, "That was him, wasn't it?"

I could do nothing but nod my head as I slumped onto the couch.

"Son of a…" Donovan said, throwing his jacket and grabbing the phone out of my hand, "I'm going to kill him, I swear it!"

I snapped out of it. "Donovan, you can't! You have to stay away from him."

He slammed the phone on the table. "What did he want?"

I repeated what Michael said. Donovan sat on the couch next to me. "That will never happen. Don't let him scare you into anything. You will NOT let him back into Constance's life. I won't allow it. He will destroy all of you and I will serve time in jail before I let that happen. Don't even think about it."

I've never seen this side of him. "Look Donovan, I am not going to let you take the fall for all of this…" He leaned over and for a second I thought he was going to kiss me but instead he put his nose to mine and put his hand on the back of my head.

"You listen to me. This is the last time I'm going to say it so listen carefully," he said then leaned over and whispered in my ear, "You will NOT do this. Leave things alone and let the chips fall where they may. I will not let y'all be unhappy ever again if it's within my power," he kissed me on the cheek and sat back on the couch.

I looked at him irritated in more ways than one. I didn't realize I wanted him to kiss me for starters and secondly he is being so bullheaded about this whole thing. He grabbed his jacket and got up.

"Where are you going?" I asked.

He looked at me with those sparkling gray eyes. "I have some things I have to take care of."

I jumped up and grabbed his arm. "You are not going to take care of Michael."

He gave me a sheepish grin. "Who said anything about that?"

I just gazed at him, shaking my head, "Um…you did. You can't tell me, without lying to me, that's not where you were going. Thirty seconds ago you were ready to kill him and now you expect me to believe you have no intentions of going over there?"

He pulled me back over to the couch to sit. "Babe," - *There was that word again* - "I can't honestly say that I wasn't. I don't know what it is but he has figured out how to really push my buttons since you got to town. There is just something about you…" He stopped himself from finishing. "Look, Sherri, I'm just not going to let him take advantage or bully you into anything. I'll handle it."

He got up and started for the door again but in a flash I grabbed him and threw him back on the couch. His eyes widened with amazement as I stalked toward him.

CHAPTER 9

"Okay, now it's time to listen to me," I said. "I'm not going to sit back and let you do something stupid because of me. He isn't worth it and we both know it. He is just trying to get under our skin. So what do you propose we do?"

He thought about that intensely before answering, "I guess a no contact clause in the restraining order means nothing. We can change your numbers but he will still find a way to get to you. He seems to think he isn't doing anything wrong. I'm going to handle this and you can't stop me."

He got up off the couch and headed for the door again. I quickly moved and leaned back against the door, placing myself between him and it. "You're not going anywhere, Donovan. If you want out you'll have to go through me."

He started laughing. "So what, you're going to hold me hostage?"

I hadn't looked at it from that perspective. I started laughing also. "Well, I guess if that's what I have to do."

He put his hand over my shoulder on the door and got really close. "So, what if I promise not to go anywhere near him?"

He was so close I could just lean forward a little and have my lips on his. I reprimanded myself and snapped back to reality. "You said you wouldn't lie to me and breaking a promise is just as bad as lying. So if you promise not to go anywhere near him and to walk the other way if you see him then I will let you leave. Otherwise, I will be stuck to you like glue until we leave for the tour. Once I know we are nowhere near him I will let you have your space."

I could practically see the wheels in his head turning.

110

He slammed his hand into the door next to my head and I winced. "GOD! I just can't do it. I can't make that promise because I know I will break it the minute I walk out that door."

He pulled me into him. "I'm so sorry I scared you. I would never put a hand on you. I'm nothing like him I can promise you that."

We stood there in an embrace and I was lost in his essence when Steph walked in. "I heard all the noise. Is everything okay?"

We let go and I tried not to look at her. "Yeah everything is fine. We will be having a houseguest for a while. I'm going to grab him a pillow and blanket," I said and excused myself.

Donovan was on the couch and I was in my bed and once again couldn't sleep. I wanted to go watch television but I didn't want to wake him. I tossed and turned for over an hour and finally couldn't stand it anymore. I went in the living room and he was lying on the couch with a blanket pulled up to his chin but wide-awake.

"I'm sorry. My couch probably isn't as comfortable as your bed at home," I offered while I grabbed the remote.

"No, it's actually not that bad. I just can't seem to wind down."

I turned the television on. "Yeah, I can't seem to sleep either. Television usually helps. It won't bother you, will it?" I asked as I sat down in the chair.

"Actually," he said, "It's been so long since I could just sit down and watch television it would really be nice to. Might help me get my mind off of things but this couch is more comfortable than that chair if you want to sit over here."

I opened my mouth and before I could stop it I was turning him down, "That's okay. Thank you, though. You look really comfortable and if you're going to go to sleep you don't need to do it sitting up."

Smooth Sherri, real smooth. That sounded as lame coming out of my mouth as I know it sounded to him but it was too late to take it back.

He gave me a smile that made me want to die. "There is another solution, you know." I gave him a questioning look and waited. "I can put my head in your lap," he said.

I don't know what I am thinking. He is trying to get me on the couch and I seem to be coming up with reasons not to be close to him. "That won't work," I said. "I can't have someone's head in my lap without playing in their hair and I don't want things to be awkward between us."

"The only way things would be awkward between us is if you tried to rape me," he said laughing as he sat up and patted the couch. The blanket fell pooling around his waist and I noticed he didn't have a shirt on.

Oh my God! Where have you been hiding that sexy body?

I sat down and he put his head in my lap. We agreed on something to watch and I started running my hands through his hair. *Even his hair is sexy. Why am I fighting this with every ounce of me? Oh that's right, because I was a really huge idiot over a guy just over a week ago and if I get personally involved it clouds my judgment.*

I'm so deep in thought I didn't realize he was fast asleep. I, very carefully, got up, laid his head on the couch, and turned for my room. He gently grabbed my arm. "Lay here with me. Just for a little bit, please."

I bend down next to him. "But Donovan, the couch isn't big enough for the both of us."

He moved as far to the back of the couch as he could get without letting go of my arm. I didn't have a choice but to lie down but it will be okay since I'm only going to lie here for a minute.

The next thing I knew the sun was up and I was alone on the couch. *If he left I'll never forgive him.* I got up and headed for the kitchen to get some breakfast cooked but first I was going to call Donovan and let him know how unhappy I was with him. I dialed the last number and as it started ringing I could hear a cell phone ringing off in the distance. I let it ring until I found the source. Donovan's cell phone was sitting on a table on the back porch.

I looked around and spotted Donovan sitting on the beach, a sight that would melt an iceberg. He sat there shirtless, glistening his tan, muscular body with the first rays of the sun. A Kodak moment if I've ever seen one.

I started out to him. He turned and I felt my knees go weak, my heart skip a beat, and I couldn't catch my breath. *Get a hold of yourself woman.* I regained my composure and keep going. He flashed me a smile that made me feel like I was in a movie and I should just go running and kiss him. *Snap out of it! I'm mad at him right now, but just look at him.* My thoughts were driving me crazy. I stopped where I was and sat down. *That's right, he can come to me. Maybe by then I will have some sense about me.*

He interrupted my mental tirade. "Morning, babe. I hope you slept okay. I slept like a baby thanks to you. I haven't had someone put me to sleep like that in years."

Remember, you're still mad at him, I keep telling myself. "I woke up and you were gone. I figured you snuck out after I went to sleep."

He walked over and helped me up. "I wouldn't do that. You expected me here when you got up and I wouldn't have been anywhere else. When I got up you were sleeping and so beautiful I was inspired and came out on the beach to write."

We walked back to the house. "So, you're working on a new song?"

"Yeah. When inspiration strikes I have to get it on

113

paper or I might lose it," he said. He draped his arm around my shoulder and asked, "So babe, you cooking me breakfast?"

I laughed. "Well, even the warden has to feed the prisoners."

He started trying to tickle me. "So, what's for breakfast warden?"

Before I could say anything the kids came running out the back door hollering for breakfast.

Constance and Donovan were working on their song after breakfast when the phone rang. I stopped in my tracks and so did Donovan.

"Give me the phone," he demanded.

Luckily, it was just Joe. He called to give me the details about the party. "Who is coming with you?" he asked. "You can bring whoever you would like. I'm just trying to get a head count."

I turned and looked at Donovan. "I guess it will be all of us plus one if that's okay."

"That will be awesome. See you tomorrow so we can get started."

The next day we arrived at Joe's house, or I guess I should say mansion, and the kids raced to the door. We knocked and Joe opened the door and stared. "Hey Donovan. I didn't expect to see you, man. So, is this your new girlfriend?" He asked wriggling his eyebrows.

Donovan put his arm around me and replied, "Shockingly no, not yet anyway." What did he mean by that? Doesn't matter. I don't have time to fool with that right now. I have to bring my 'A' game tonight so I need all my concentration. "Michael really did a number on her."

Joe cocked his head. "Oh, Michael. How did I not know that? He's bad news for sure."

Joe invited us in and gave us the grand tour. He told Constance and Donovan if they needed or wanted to work on their music they were welcome to use his studio then showed Drew and Charlie to the playroom, which happened to be more like a football field, where they would be occupied for hours. He took me to the kitchen and showed me around then gave me everything I asked for and the money for the food.

With everyone occupied and money in hand, I headed for the market.

As we were walking to the car leaving Joe's Constance was bouncing and laughing.

"What is so funny sweetie?" I asked.

She kept laughing. "I can't tell you, Mom. It's a BIG surprise. Donovan said you would like it. I hope you do. It's really special."

I looked as he told Constance, "Don't tell her sweet pea. Not even a hint. It's a surprise and we don't want to spoil it."

I just smiled at the both of them. It's so nice to see her so happy and it doesn't matter what it is, coming from my daughter I'm sure I will love it.

The next morning I was up early with a lot to do. The big party was tonight and I have to get all the food done and ready to serve. As I was preparing the food in the kitchen the phone rang.

"Hello?" I said hesitantly.

It's Joe. "Make sure you bring something to wear tonight. I would like to introduce you to a few people if you don't mind." I agreed and told him I would see him later.

When the party started Donovan was in the kitchen talking to me.

"Don't you want to join the party out there?" I asked eliciting a smile from him.

"I will go out when you do warden," he said and we both started laughing.

"Okay. Everything is ready to go. I guess I should go change." I grabbed my bag and headed toward the bathroom. He got up and followed me.

"What are you doing?" I asked.

"Well you said I had to be glued to you and I don't know if Michael is here so I just thought I would come with you."

I pushed him out of the bathroom laughing. "Go sit down and wait on me."

The party is not a bunch of kids like I thought it would be. It's mostly agents, producers, and managers. Joe introduced me to several people and I started to notice a pattern. Every time I met someone they complimented me on the food.

I pulled Joe to the side. "Is there something you need to tell me?"

He looked puzzled and asked, "Whatever do you mean?"

We both laughed. "You know what I mean."

He patted me on the back. "I know you say you're not ready for this but you are too talented not to. It's a business you can do when you're not on the road with Constance and I think you will be really successful. You should at least give it a shot."

Maybe he was right. I don't have to take things if I don't have the time but I always have such a problem saying no. I could always teach Steph and let her take it while I'm gone. Now there's an idea.

"Thanks for pushing me, Joe. I think I just might do that."

There is so much to do before we leave for the tour. At least this tour won't take us out of the country. If we forget something we can always run out and grab it. We spent the next few days getting everything together and then it's to Donovan's house to get all of his stuff together. I'm so busy I don't have time to worry about anything else except, of course, making sure Steph and the kids are taken care of while we are gone.

We left at midnight on our way to our first stop of many, Minneapolis, Minnesota. Constance was so excited she was literally bouncing off the walls of the bus. Donovan told her all about their first show together, how excited he was, and how awesome it was going to be. It's like I have two kids instead of one. She finally calmed down and passed out.

He walked back to where I was and plopped down in the seat next to me. "So are you ready for this?"

I look at him smiling. "I probably won't ever be ready for this. Why are you back here with me? Aren't you tired of me yet? I paroled you the minute we cleared the city limits."

He leaned over and put his head on my shoulder. "I was kind of hoping maybe you could help me go to sleep." He looked up at me with those gorgeous eyes and added, "Please."

I started laughing. "Really? Have I spoiled you already? Just how am I supposed to do that? You can't tell me you're going to lie across this bar and sleep comfortably."

He stood up, motioned for me to get up, and when I did he turned the two chairs into a couch. "Voila!" he exclaimed as he sat down and patted the couch. "Will this work?"

I started laughing as I sat down. "You're incorrigible," I said as he put his head in my lap. I started running my hands through his hair. Staring out the window I let my mind wander.

What would it be like to actually be with another man that only wanted my family to be happy? What is it going to be like being on this tour? Is this really the life I want my daughter to have? Would Jonathan be proud of me and the way I have handled things? What is Minnesota going to be like?

My thoughts were interrupted when I heard, "You're not going to be able to sleep sitting like that babe."

"I'm not tired to be honest. I'm too wired to sleep, but thank you for worrying about me."

He smiled up at me. "I'll always worry about you and your family."

I chuckled. "Yeah, it would take a chunk out of your pocket if something happened to Constance."

He sat straight up and looked at me. "Are you really serious right now? You honestly think everything I have been doing was all because of money? I thought you knew me better than that." He got up and walked to the front of the bus where he sat down and stared out of the window.

Why did I say that? Why do the wrong things always come out of my mouth?

I walked up, put my hand on his shoulder, and started to say I was sorry but he shrugged my hand off of him. "I'm sorry. I really am. I didn't mean to offend you in any way. I just can't seem to ever find the right thing to say." He wouldn't even look at me.

I walked back and laid down miserable with myself. He has really been good to us but I can't help but remember Michael being so helpful. I have to stop comparing him to Michael or this tour is going to be miserable for all of us.

"Babe, wake up." I slowly opened my eyes and Donovan was standing over me. "We're at the hotel. Do you want to go get some sleep or would you rather go sightseeing?"

I sat up. "Don't we have a concert in a few hours?"

He took my hand and helped me up. "No, they had to postpone it because a roof collapsed or something. They have to line us up in another venue so we have a day to sightsee or rest up, the choice is yours."

Constance was standing behind him. "Mom, I want to go see some stuff."

I looked at him and smiled. "Well, I guess sightseeing is on our list for today."

We went to our rooms to get freshened up and changed. As we walked into our room I was shocked. I have never seen a room like this. It's a suite and it takes up half the floor. We have a separate living room, bedroom, and kitchen. It is absolutely amazing.

Shortly there was a knock at the door. "Y'all ready to go?" Donovan asked as he slowly opened the door. "We have a limo waiting out front. We have to get going before the paparazzi realize we're here."

Our first stop is the Mall of America. There is a huge theme park right in the middle of it. Constance was going crazy. She wants to ride all the rides, of course.

"Constance, we don't have the money for all of that and besides you really don't want to ride alone."

Donovan laughed. "I will get the tickets and there is no way she would have to ride alone." He came back with tickets and another little girl Constance's age. "All set," he told them. The girls got on a ride and I turned to him.

"How did you do that? Did you just kidnap some random child to ride with her?" I asked laughing.

"No, all I had to do was ask. You forget, I'm a celebrity," he said jokingly.

It is wonderful seeing Constance having so much fun but I can't just forget about what happened last night. I took his hand. "About last night –"

He stopped me and kissed me gently on the cheek. "All is forgiven and forgotten. Life is too short to have regrets. I'm sorry for turning my back on you but I had a song running through my head and I had to get it straight and on paper before I lost it. No worries, babe."

We left the mall and headed for the new venue. Donovan wanted to check out the acoustics to make sure everything would work. There will only be one quick run-through tomorrow before the show.

Back at the hotel he told me, "If you want or need anything at all I'm just a call away and so is room service. Whatever you need, I'll take care of." He kissed me on the cheek and headed out the door.

About an hour or so later Constance was on her bed passed out with all the stuffed animals Donovan won her and I, of course, couldn't sleep. I heard a light tap at the door.

I got up and went to door, cracking it open enough to see Donovan. "I didn't wake you did I?" he asked.

"No, you know from staying with me that I rarely sleep."

He smiled. "Yeah, I can't sleep either. Guess I have gotten a little spoiled. I was thinking maybe we could watch some television like we did before and it might help both of us sleep, " he said grinning.

"I know what you're up to but I'm not going to say no. Come on in."

We snuggled on the couch watching television with me running my fingers through his hair.

Constance woke us up.

"Wow, I can't believe I actually slept here all night," Donovan said, embarrassed that Constance caught us asleep together. "I'm going to my suite to grab a shower and then we will get some breakfast before our run-through if you want."

We agreed to meet him downstairs in about thirty minutes. He left and the door wasn't closed well before Constance came over to me giggling. "Mom, do you like Donovan?"

I started blushing. "Now Constance, of course I like Donovan."

She started laughing. "No mom, I mean the way you liked daddy."

That caught me off guard. I really hadn't given it much thought. *I mean I liked Donovan, but I am pretty sure I didn't love him or wasn't in love with him, but at the same time I could definitely fall in love with him if I allowed myself the chance.*

"No Constance, I don't love him like I did your daddy but I do like him."

She pressed for more, "Do you like him as a friend, or do you like him like him?"

"Well honey, I don't see why that matters."

Trying to act like a grownup she said, "Because mom if you like him like him, you should tell him, cause I think he likes you likes you."

My turn to press. "Did he tell you that he likes me likes me?" I asked, sounding like a child and starting to feel like one back in grade school.

"No mom, he won't tell me just like you won't, but I think he does. So do you like him like him mom?"

I bent down, "Can you keep a secret? I think I do like him like him but you can't tell him. Pinky swear?"

She pinky swore. "I'm good at keeping secrets. I still haven't told you about mine and Donovan's secret," she said laughing.

The rehearsal went well. Donovan has an amazing voice and stage presence and I think Constance can learn a lot from him. With everything set we headed back to the hotel.

Once we were back in the limo Donovan took my hand and said, "So…that dinner. I think I'm ready to collect."

Chapter 10

Donovan smiled at my apparent apprehension and explained, "The band wants to take Constance out for a celebratory dinner so I was thinking if it was okay with you that we would have the dinner you owe me tonight."

As mean as I had been to him lately I didn't have the heart to say no, even though I was exhausted. "Sure, I guess that would be fine. What should I wear?"

"Whatever you wear to the concert will be fine. It won't be anything fancy, just dinner."

I had butterflies in my stomach worrying about Constance and this concert. She, on the other hand, was bouncing off the walls and not the least bit nervous. I wished I could be her age again. The concert started and I stood right off stage watching Donovan perform while Constance was being waited on hand and foot. He is so amazing. Why had I never see it before?

With it almost time for Constance to go on I was more and more nervous but she didn't seem to be phased. Donovan announced he would be doing a duet and introduced Constance. They were wonderful together. The concert went perfectly and Constance got a standing ovation. I was so proud I could burst. Donovan went back on stage as the crowd was chanting "ENCORE!! ENCORE!!" Constance and Donovan did another duet and the crowd still wanted more. Donovan said they would love to but that the crowd should instead buy a CD and promised to be back for another show very soon. He then did something I never expected. He called me out on the stage. "Let's give a big round of applause for the person that gave us Constance, her beautiful mother and manager, Sherri."

I also received a standing ovation. This is out of this

world. I have never felt so loved or adored. My kid's dreams are going to come true. Constance is on top of the world. I got her ready to go with the band and my phone went off. It was a text from Donovan.

I am on the top floor at the hotel. When you get off the elevator you will know where to go. Go in the bathroom and relax in a bubble bath and I will get there as soon as I can. I have an autograph session but I promise not to be too long.

I felt weird going up to his room alone but that's what he asked and since I owed him I'd do it. I got to the top floor at the hotel and when the elevator doors opened there on the floor was a path of rose petals leading to a door that was slightly cracked open. When I pushed the door open there was a strange man standing there.

"Ms. Sherri?" the guy asked.

I didn't really want to tell this guy who I was but surely Donovan knew he was here. "Yes?"

He walked over and took my hand, "Your bath waits."

He led me to the bathroom and excused himself. I opened the bathroom door and there were a million candles everywhere, a tub full of bubbles, and a glass of champagne next to the tub. I felt like a princess.

I was soaking in the tub when my phone went off again, startling me, with another text from Donovan.

I hope everything is to your satisfaction. Will be there soon. Enjoy yourself until I see you.

I was in the tub for what seemed like forever but finally able to relax for once in a long time when I heard a knock on the door. "Babe, are you decent? Can I come in?"

I was covered in bubbles so he couldn't see anything. "Yes, come on in."

Donovan brought in a menu. "Order anything you want and it's yours."

I figured out what I wanted to eat and told him. As he

walked out he said, "Take your time. It will take room service time to get the food up here. I'm glad you're relaxing. You need and deserve it. I will knock on the door when the food gets here and you can get out then. There is a silk robe hanging next to the tub for you."

A few minutes later there was a knock at the door. "Food is here, babe. You can get out now if you want," Donovan said laughing.

I started letting the water out and waited for every drop of water to drain before I finally got out. I get out and put on the robe, which was so soft I almost get lost in its silky quality. *Snap back to earth Sherri, Donovan is waiting.* I walked out of the bathroom and into the living room to find the entire room surrounded by candles. There are rose petals all over the entire living room floor and soft music playing in the background. The table is set with two candles, food, and a bottle of champagne.

Donovan walked over and handed me a single red rose. "This is nowhere near as beautiful as you," he said and kissed me on the cheek. I felt like royalty. He pulled my chair out. "Shall we eat beautiful?"

I knew I was grinning from ear to ear but I couldn't help myself. As we sat I said, "This is all too much, Donovan."

He took my hand. "Nothing is too much when it comes to you, babe. Your every wish is my command," he said as he kissed my hand.

"But, Donovan, I still don't understand why. You didn't have to go through all of this trouble."

He looked at me with nothing but compassion in his eyes. "I still can't tell you. If I do I might scare you off. Just know that I only have the best of intentions for you and your family."

I stopped myself before I said 'yeah I've heard that before'. "I'm sorry for being so skeptical, but look at

125

everything that has happened since I got to that stupid state. Yes, my daughter is happy but at whose expense?"

He stood up and pulled me up to him. "Sherri, the only thing I could have done to stop it before it started was stalking you before you even got there. I'm so sorry you had to go through all of that and I wish I could change it all, but I can't. You will see that I'm not him and nothing like him and only want what's best for y'all. Look, let's not talk or think about it tonight. Tonight is all about us and I want it to stay that way, please."

"I'll try but that's the best I can offer," I replied as I sat back down to eat. He sat also and we ate while making small talk.

"Do you want dessert babe?"

I smiled at him. "I couldn't eat anything else. It was delicious though. Thank you for all of this. I really needed some down time."

He stood up and reached his hand out, "It's not over yet. Unless of course you want it to be."

I took his hand and he snapped his fingers. Music started playing softly in the background. "Dance with me?"

I started laughing. "Here? Now?"

He pulled me to him. "Why not?"

"I guess there is really no reason."

We slow danced and our eyes stayed locked on one another. I could see what I thought were genuine feelings for me but I have been wrong before. I didn't know what to think but I was enjoying myself so I was just going to go with it. As I looked into his eyes he leaned over and put his nose to mine.

"Sherri, I know you don't know me that well but you need to know one thing about me. I don't want anything from you that you aren't willing to give. I hope in time you will see that I'm truly a genuine and honest guy. I only want happiness for you and your family."

126

I prepared myself for the kiss that I knew was coming. I wanted him to kiss me to be honest. He pulled me to him and we danced a while longer. *Okay, maybe I read this wrong. I thought he was going to kiss me.* I found myself a little disappointed. As much as I wanted him to maybe it's for the best. I didn't know if I was ready to trust another Hollywood movie star so soon. The music went off but we kept dancing. I didn't know if he even realized it.

"Donovan?"

He looked at me and smiled. "I'm sorry. I was really enjoying the dance, was hoping you wouldn't notice the music went off. Would you like to dance some more?"

I shrugged. "It really doesn't matter to me, I don't guess."

He left the room and the music came back on. He returned and took my hand. "I have a better idea."

He sat on the bed and patted next to him for me to do the same. I felt like a prude when I said, "I'm not going to sleep with you Donovan."

He laughed. "I had no intentions of trying anything. Just trust me and if I do anything you don't approve of you feel free to tell me."

I didn't sleep with Michael and I have no intentions of sleeping with Donovan either. That just adds drama to an already drama-filled situation. We sat on the bed and he started massaging my shoulders. *Oh good lord I am in heaven.* As he massaged my shoulders he gently kissed my neck. It sure looked to me like he was trying to start something but I was beginning not to care anymore. My whole body tingled. He moved the robe off my shoulders slightly and continued to massage while gently moving his kisses from my neck to my shoulders. I could feel my body melting under his touch.

As he kissed my shoulders I heard a familiar voice. Jonathan. "Sherri, you have a right to be happy. You have been hurt and now it's your time to be happy. Don't deny yourself this. I can tell you he is a stand-up guy. I love you and always will, but you have to move on."

"I love you too," I said.

Donovan stopped massaging. "What did you say?"

I was beyond petrified. "I'm sorry. I said I love this." I think I covered that quite well but I wasn't entirely convinced he bought it. He was looking at me so intently that I decided to distract him. I leaned over and kissed him ever so gently on the lips. He looked even more shocked than he was before.

That's just great, now I have really made an ass out of myself. He didn't want me to kiss him. Jeez Sherri! What the hell were you thinking?

"I'm sorry...I..." I stammered. As I jumped up to run to the bathroom and away from him he grabbed my arm. He stood to face me and I tried again to apologize and get away from the awkwardness. "I'm so...."

He kissed me more passionately than I had ever been kissed. I was so lost in it that it seemed to go on forever but I wasn't complaining. Without stopping the kiss he gently picked me up and laid me on the bed. The longer the kiss lasted the more I could feel the stress pouring out of my body. It's almost like his touch turns me to Jell-O. He pulled away from me.

"I'm sorry, Sherri. I have wanted to do that since the first day I laid eyes on you. I didn't mean to get so carried away."

I smiled up at him. "I wasn't complaining and I didn't tell you to stop."

"But you said..."

I leaned up and stopped him by kissing him. I lightly bit his lip. "It's okay. I know what I said but I think I was wrong."

He laughed. "You think? I don't want you to think you

128

were wrong, I want you to know it. I don't want you to have any regrets. I want you to be sure this is what you want before anything at all happens between us."

I gazed into his amazing gray eyes. "I'm sure."

He leaned over and kissed me, moving his kisses from my lips down my body and then back up. He didn't stop until he had kissed every inch of me. He ran his fingers delicately over me in a way that made me go numb with anticipation. He was so gentle and caring that I knew my decision was the right one. We made love slowly and tenderly until the sun came up; soaking each other up until every drop of energy was gone. We lay there wrapped in each other's arms. There is no way to explain it but it felt so right.

The phone rang and Donovan answered it. When he hung up the phone he said, "That was Jay, the drummer. He said they are going to take Constance out for some breakfast and for us to meet them downstairs in about two hours." He rolled over and put his arm around me. "Should we get up and have some breakfast or do you want to stay in bed?"

I smiled and snuggled into his arms. "I don't want to move."

"Sounds perfect to me."

The phone rang, waking us up. "Babe, they are waiting on us downstairs. We have to get up and get going."

I rolled over. "I thought we weren't leaving until this afternoon."

He smiled. "We aren't, but I always go and make sure everything gets loaded and taken care of. I'm kind of anal like that. But if you want to stay here and sleep you are welcome to. I can come back and get you when we get done."

I thought about it but I hadn't seen my daughter since

129

her concert last night and I really didn't want to pawn her off on anyone any longer. "No, that's okay. I'll come with you. I'm dying to see Constance anyway."

The elevator door opened and Constance came running. "Mom, I missed you but I had SO much fun with these guys. I hope you and Donovan had a good night without me."

Donovan leaned over and tousled her hair. "It's never as much fun if you're not there, sweet pea, but I think we managed just fine."

The band hugged me and welcomed me to the family. I guess this was how they treated everyone. They all seem so nice. They were all smiling and congratulating Donovan. I guess it was a pretty awesome show last night but they did some of the work so I started congratulating them and they all looked at me crazy.

The bus was loaded and I grabbed the last of my things from the room. Donovan was already loaded and on the bus. I have to learn how he does that so fast. I got everything packed and loaded and boarded the bus. Donovan made us a makeshift bed in the back and I was so thankful. I was totally exhausted and drained from the night before. I might not be cut out for life on the road.

We lay down and Constance crawled in the bed right between us. Donovan smiled at me, puts his arm around both of us, and we all fell asleep. We woke up in Green Bay, Wisconsin. After the fiasco in Minneapolis we had to be ready for a show tonight with very little time to spare. Donovan had the bus drop us off at the hotel so that we could get a shower and freshen up and then it's on to the coliseum to get ready for the show.

Once at the coliseum Donovan went into full on manic mode running around trying to make sure everything was going to be ready. Constance and I were led to her dressing room. Constance was being doted on like a princess. She has people buzzing all around her doing her nails, hair, makeup, etc. There was a knock at the door followed by, "Constance, Sherri, can I come in?"

"Yeah, Donovan, come on in." He came in and looked like he had just won a Grammy. His smile is so big that his eyes look like they are going to pop out of his head. I wondered what has him so excited.

"Donovan, what's going on?"

He walked over to us. "I have good news and bad news. Which do you want first?"

I started laughing. "Well normally I would say bad news but something has you grinning like a mule eating briars so this time I'll have to say the good news."

He took Constance's hand and my hand. "Mr. James called a little bit ago. The good news is Constance sold over two thousand albums at last night's show and they are already requesting her songs on the radio."

Constance jumped out of her chair, messing up her makeup and hair, and started dancing around. I was so shocked I could barely speak.

I finally muttered up the words, "And the bad news?"

He turned his attention to me. "Well, the bad news isn't really all that bad to be honest. I have to be in court next week for trial. So, we will have to postpone the rest of the tour for a couple of weeks."

Constance stopped dancing. "Postpone? But I'm just getting started. The people love me already. I will lose them if I don't keep going."

Donovan knelt down on one knee. "Constance, they aren't going to forget about you. Trust me; they will be right here waiting when we get back." She seemed to be eased by hearing this.

He stood up. "So Sherri, how do you feel about PDA?" he asked laughing.

131

I was taken by surprise. Apparently he wanted a kiss in front of my daughter. I smiled. "It's not a problem, I don't suppose." He smiled, kissed me on the cheek, and said he would see us on stage.

What the? Okay, I guess he didn't want a kiss in front of Constance. Now he was giving me mixed signals and I wasn't sure what to think. I thought last night meant as much to him as it did me but apparently I misread the situation. It's okay. Just have to play it cool, Sherri.

The concert went just like the last one with the exception of the duet. It was a song I had never heard before and not the one I heard them working on. Listening to the words I thought this could be the song he had been working on since the morning I found him on the beach but it would be egotistical of me to assume this song was about me.

My heart and mind are in a prison
The walls are holding me captive
But being with you I'm learning all over again how to
live
You have been hurt before, it's true
The only thing I want from you is to let me love you.
You have been the light in my eyes since I first saw you.
I'm being real and I hope you see it's true.
I want nothing from you but your happiness and faith
And I'm willing to wait as long as it takes

With that the concert ended. Donovan thanked everyone. "And now for the lady that brought us this little miracle, Sherri come on out."

I wasn't surprised this time. Apparently this was going to be a regular thing at the end of the shows. He had his hand stretched out and I took it. He pulled me in and kissed me in front of all those people and then announced, "Just so there is no confusion or rumors floating around out there, Sherri and I are dating," he paused and looked at me, "that is, if she will have me."

I was completely embarrassed but in a good way. I wasn't sure what to say and I hadn't given it much thought but I couldn't leave him hanging in front of all these people. "Yes, Donovan, I'll date you."

He kissed me again and the crowd went wild. I felt like a kid in grade school who just got one of those notes "Do you like me? Check yes or no."

Constance broke my train of thought. "MOMMA, MOMMA, MOMMA!!! Did you like your surprise? Donovan wrote it for us but said you would know why and would love it. Didn't you just love it, mom?"

Donovan walked up behind her. "Calm down, sweet pea. You haven't given her a chance to say anything."

They both looked at me with questioning looks. "I loved it. Thank you," I said hugging them both. "Is that the song you were writing on the beach that morning?" I asked Donovan.

He took me in his arms. "Yes, it is. I hope you did really like it. I really put my heart into it." I kissed him passionately. "WOW," he said, "I guess I got my answer."

Chapter 11

Constance and I were in the dressing room winding down, or trying to anyway, when there was another knock on the door. "Sherri, Constance, we have to hit the road in an hour. We have to make it to New York City in two days." It was Danny, the piano player.

"We'll be there," I shouted. We got to the buses and Donovan had arranged for Constance to ride with the band because he and I needed to talk apparently.

"Donovan, I can't believe you put me on the spot like that," I said and he kissed me.

"I'm sorry but I was worried if I didn't do it in front of all those people you would tell me no."

I started laughing. "Honestly, I don't know what my answer would have been but more than likely it would have still been yes."

"That's not what I wanted to talk to you about. I mean that's important but this is more important. Constance was very upset about having to postpone the tour so I hired a private jet to be on standby for the two weeks we will be having trial that way we won't have to postpone the tour at all. It's going to be very hectic but we can do it."

I didn't know what to say. He did this all for Constance and I was very stunned. "Donovan, that had to cost you a fortune. You didn't have to do that."

He gently ran his hand along my cheek. "No, I know I didn't, but I told you before and I will tell you again, I will do anything it takes to make you and your family happy. Money is nothing to me and if I can use it to make y'all happy that's what I'll do."

I was about to object when my phone rang. "Hello?"

"Well hello, sweetheart," - Michael, of course – "I guess you weren't expecting to hear from me but you should have known I wasn't going to give you up without a

134

fight."

"Look Michael…" but before I could say anything else Donovan grabbed the phone.

"Look, I'm sure you know by now what happened tonight and if you don't leave the future mother of my children alone I will see to it that you never work in that town again."

I stared at him as he hung up the phone. "What –"

He cut me off. "I'm sorry, Sherri. I shouldn't have said that but if he thinks we are serious maybe he will back off." He smiled at me and added, "But you have to admit if we had kids together they would be unstoppable in Hollywood."

I didn't even want to think about what just happened. "I need sleep, Donovan. You might be used to all this excitement but I'm not and I have to get some rest." We were both so exhausted we slept all the way to New York.

The next week flew by. Everything was so hectic that Donovan and I didn't have any time to be alone but at the end of every show he doesn't hesitate to announce to the world that he and I are an item. After our Tallahassee show we boarded the jet heading back to California. We had to be in court the next morning. It will be great to be able to sleep in my own bed.

We arrived home to find the paparazzi camped out on my lawn. "Welcome to stardom, babe," Donovan said laughing. The boys and Steph were ecstatic to see us. Everybody was talking a hundred miles a minute. Finally everyone calmed down and Donovan put the kids in bed answering a thousand questions on the way.

"So the phone has been ringing off the hook since you left, Sherri. People are wanting to book you to do everything from parties to benefit concerts. I didn't know what to tell them."

"I'm too tired to even think right now. Talk to

Donovan and find out when the tour will be over and you can start booking two weeks after that. Only book for six months after that though because I have no idea what's going to happen next."

Steph smiled at me. "So, are you too tired to fill me in on Donovan? It's been pretty interesting around here and you know I HATE not knowing what's going on."

"Well Steph, I would love to tell you but I'm not even sure myself."

I started to tell her everything when Donovan came in the room. "Well babe, I guess I'm headed home. Need to get some sleep before court in the morning. Meet you there?"

I stood up and grabbed his arm, "Now you hold it right there mister. Your parole has been revoked. You're under house arrest while we are in this town until all of this is settled."

He grinned. "Oh, is that right?"

"Well yes, that's right. I'm the warden and I am not going to let the future father of my children go do something stupid that will land him in jail so you're under house arrest while we're here."

He laughed and put his hands out in front of him. "So, are you going to handcuff me? I didn't know you liked it rough, babe."

Steph jumped up. "Oh my God! I did NOT need to hear all of that. One of you is going to tell me what's going on before I explode."

We gave Steph the short version and went to bed. Tomorrow morning was going to come early.

As we walked in the courthouse we saw that Michael was already there with his lawyer. He walked toward us and I stepped in between him and Donovan.

"So Donovan, you drop the charges and I will do the

same. We can work everything out afterwards."

Donovan started to say something but I put my hand over his mouth. "Now you listen here Michael. I'm done with this and so is he. If you try to have any further contact with my family or me then I will see to it you are run out of town and are exposed for the cheating, child beater that you are. Now leave all of us alone and that will be the last time it's said."

Michael extended his hand like he expected Donovan to shake it. "Well then, may the best man win."

Donovan moved toward him but I stopped him. "Donovan, just leave it alone. I'm not going to date a man that's behind bars, no matter how good the reason."

As we turned to walk off Donovan couldn't resist, "The best man has won. I have the girl and the life."

What does he mean by that? Am I a prize now? Definitely a conversation we will have but it'll have to wait until after court. The day went in our favor, but that's just my opinion.

"Babe, we have just enough time to run by the house, grab Constance, and say bye to the boys before we have to be back on the jet so we can make it to Pensacola and get a little sleep before our next concert."

"Okay, Donovan. We need to talk before we get Constance. What was all that with Michael? I am NOBODY'S trophy, I'm not a possession, and I won't be a prize between you and him. You have me because I thought you really liked me but had I known it was just a way to get even with him I never would have agreed. I really like you a lot but I think we should just end this relationship now before me or my family end up hurt. I will not do this to them again."

He turned to me and took my hand. "You're right," he said, "It's time we had an adult conversation. We haven't had a lot of time to talk and I'm sorry for that but I think it's time for you to know the whole story and why I have done everything I have done. First, all that with Michael was not what you think it was. I am not in competition with him but he has been in competition with me since I first saw you. It's a game to him and I said that in the heat of the moment. You're not a trophy or my possession, not at all. It's time you know the whole story. My girlfriend at the time called me and told me I just had to see this video that was going viral on the Internet. I turned on the video and you're going to think I'm lying, which is why I haven't told you this before, but when the video started I didn't see anyone but you. My heart literally stopped beating for two seconds. I had to start the video over so I could watch Constance to be honest. I heard her, but I could only look at you. I knew then that I wanted you. While I was watching the video the second time is when Michael saw it. He informed me he was going to have you and Constance all to himself. I tried to stop it, I swear to you, but it was too late. All I could do was wait until you were here and try to stop the avalanche. I'm sorry I didn't try harder. You were a trophy to him but never to me. I called my girlfriend that day and told her I couldn't see her anymore. I haven't noticed another woman since. Please don't end this. I don't want to think about any of this without you."

I was speechless. I didn't have a clue what to say to that. I wasn't sure if I believed it but if it weren't true then why would he do all of the stuff he has done. He did try to warn me about Michael but I didn't give him the time of day. He had been straight with me this whole time and Jonathan wouldn't have told me to be happy if he knew that Donovan was a fake.

He stroked my face gently. "Say something, please, babe."

I leaned over and kissed him, "We're okay. I'm sorry for overreacting but you can ask Steph, that's my specialty.

But no more cracks to Michael like that or I will have to put you in your place in front of all those people."

"Anything if it means keeping you by my side."

Flying back and forth was starting to take its toll on all of us. Luckily the trial was starting to wrap up. It was great to see the boys while we were on tour but we were all exhausted. We left from Memphis for our last day of testimony. After that we were just waiting on a verdict. He could tour while they were making their decision and if they found him guilty he would have twenty-four hours to turn himself in. Mr. Johnson said things were looking good for us. He also told us that he managed to get Michael's trial moved to after the tour was over. I was really glad to hear that because touring was hard enough but the extra stress of having to be in court was almost not worth it.

We flew into Phoenix for the concert that night. It was the last flight for a while unless he was found guilty. The concerts were all awesome with each ending the same way. I wasn't so sure what I thought of life in the spotlight but I guessed I might as well get used to it.

Our next stop was Seattle, Washington. The last stop before we could go home. Constance was ready and we were headed to the stage when Donovan walked up. "Constance, go ahead. I need to talk to your mom for a minute."

He looked worried. I started to freak out as usual. "What happened? What's going on? Are the boys okay? Did something happen to Steph?"

"Slow down, Sherri, I can't keep up. Mr. Johnson called. Did you really mean what you said about not wanting to date a man in jail?"

My eyes filled with tears. "They have a verdict and it's not good?"

He pulled me in to hug me. "Oh Sherri, I'm so sorry. I

was just picking with you. They found me not guilty."

I jerked away from him and hit him. "Don't you EVER do that to me again. That was just not right!"

He hugged and kissed me. "I'm sorry, babe. I just wanted to see if you really cared. I promise not to ever do that to you again. I do have even better news, but we need Constance before I can tell you."

We walked toward the stage where Constance was waiting to perform. "Constance," Donovan started, "You are going to be so excited when I tell you this but you have to maintain yourself because you still have a concert to put on." She nodded in agreement. "Mr. James called. You have sold over ten thousand CD's since the tour started. That's a record! But the even better news is that my record label wants to sign you. That means if you want to, when we get back to town, you will start recording your first actual album and be all on your own."

She was screaming with excitement but all of a sudden stopped. "Does that mean I won't get to tour or work with you anymore?"

He bent down and put his hand on her shoulder. "Yeah, you will be all on your own. You will have someone who tours with you and you will be the headline instead of following behind me all the time. This is great! Your career is off to a great start."

She teared up. "But I don't want to do it without you."

He hugged her. "But, sweet pea, this will get you everything you want. We can still work together sometimes."

She broke his embrace and ran off.

"I'll get her," Donovan said but there is no way I was letting him go by himself. She needs her mother. I found them in her dressing room and I was about to go in the door when I heard what Donovan said to her. "Constance, this is a great opportunity for you. You can't always follow in my shadow. You have too much talent to hide behind me the rest of your life. Don't you want to live your dream?"

She started crying. He pulled her in and hugged her. "Oh, sweet pea. What's wrong? I thought this is what you wanted."

She was on the verge of hyperventilating and I started to go in but what she said made me stop. "Donovan, I wanted to be a star but money isn't everything and I don't want to be without you. I lost one daddy and I don't want to lose you too."

He pulled her away and started wiping her tears. "Constance, I'm not your daddy, but I will always be around."

"I know you're not my daddy, but you're the closest thing I have had since my daddy died. He said he would always be here for me and now I'm living our dream and he can't even see me."

He wrapped her up in his arms again. "Constance, he is watching you. He is always watching you and what happened to him was a horrible, horrible accident. I will always be around. You will never have to be without me, I promise."

She tore away from him and went to the other side of the room with her back turned to him. "And how can you promise me that? I'm not a little girl. I know what a promise is and people break them all the time. Once I go out on my own you will be doing your shows and stuff and I won't ever see you."

He walked over and picked her up. "Look, I promised you and I will keep that promise. I don't ever want to see you sad. I will figure something out where I can make sure you get to see me at least every couple of days. I know you're old enough to know about promises and you need to know I don't make promises I can't keep."

She started to smile a little. "Pinky promise?"

He started laughing and put her down. "Pinky promise. You are so cute and I love you to pieces."

She hugged him. "Awww, I love you to pieces too, Donovan."

I walked in. "Is everything okay here?" I asked with a smile.

Constance ran over to me. "It's fine. I'm sorry for acting like a baby, mom. We have everything settled and a pinky promise in place," she said as she headed back to the stage.

Donovan started laughing. "It was the only way to calm her down."

I look at him doubtfully. "But, Donovan, she means what she says. If you break a promise to her you will break her heart."

He kissed me gently on the nose. "I have no intentions of ever breaking a promise to any of you. I don't make promises I can't keep," he assured me.

The last couple of concerts Donovan let Constance take the lead. He was preparing her to be out on her own. He is so great with her. I just hoped when the other two kids got to know him they would love him as much as Constance does. I really wanted some alone time with him too. We would be home in the next couple of days and maybe then we can all get some down time.

Our last concert in Seattle, Washington was finally over and everything was packed up. The time had come for the customary end-of-tour party. The hotel was a mob scene. There were people everywhere waiting to get in to meet Donovan, or so I thought. Turns out they were there to see Constance. Donovan told the limo driver to take us in the secret entrance so we could get in without being seen. He turned to Constance, "I would be jealous of you if I didn't have your mom to keep me entertained," he said laughing.

We went up to the suite to freshen up before we joined the party in the ballroom. Donovan explained to Constance what she should expect. "In the beginning it will be adult time. You will meet and great some of the greats behind the scenes and you have to schmooze them. It's really boring," he laughed and continued, "Then they will let in the wild crowd. I hope you're ready to sign autographs and pose for pictures. These are the most important people because they are your fans. They decide if you make it or don't in this business. Always be polite, but not overly friendly. One stalker is enough for now." He means Michael, I was sure of it. "I know you think boys are gross at this age, but you have to be nice to them too. If it gets to be too much for you just excuse yourself and come find me and your mom."

We went downstairs and there were already a lot of people in the ballroom and a line outside the hotel that went for miles. "Wow," Donovan said to Constance, "I haven't seen this many people excited to see someone in a very long time. You're going to go far in this business, young lady."

Donovan introduced us to several of the big wigs like owners of the venues, promoters, etc. Everyone told Constance what an amazing person she was and wished her well. Finally it was time to let in what Donovan called the wild crowd, which was full of kids trying to get pictures and autographs and parents that were just ready to go home. Donovan told security the easiest way to handle this was to form a line and let everyone meet Constance and then if they wanted to meet him they could. He knew most of the people there were there for Constance and it didn't bother him at all. Constance was eating up all the attention. I am really proud of how she is handling things. Several people wanted a picture of all three of us together so when a guy asked it came as nothing out of the ordinary.

He was standing on the end next to Donovan then Constance and then me. When the photo was done he asked Donovan for an autograph and mumbled something incoherently. Donovan handed him the pen back and looked at him trying to make out what he said. "What did you say? I'm sorry, I couldn't understand."

The guy looked at Donovan and screamed, "And you never will!" He took the pen and stabbed Donovan in the neck.

CHAPTER 12

Everyone started running and screaming. Security wrestled the guy to the ground while I tried to stop the bleeding from Donovan's neck. Constance grabbed a phone and called for an ambulance. The cops and ambulance arrived at the same time but Donovan was unconscious because he had lost so much blood.

As they were loading him in the ambulance the cops were talking to me. Constance stood by his side crying. "Donovan you can't leave me. You pinky promised you'd always be here. I love you. Don't leave me."

I politely told the officer, "I'm sorry sir, but any questions you have for me will have to wait. The man I love could be dying," as I climbed in the ambulance.

Did I really just tell that officer I loved Donovan? I guess it takes something like this to make me be honest with myself. I didn't even realize it until I heard it come out of my mouth.

I got in the ambulance next to Constance and Donovan and took his hand. "Donovan, don't you leave me now. We need you. You have to hang in there."

At the hospital the admittance people asked me tons of questions I didn't know the answers to as they were rushing him to surgery. His next of kin, his date of birth, his blood type. Luckily Danny and the rest of the band got there and Danny had the answers they were looking for.

The hospital was a mad house. Security was screening people and only letting in staff and people needing medical attention.

Danny came over to us. "I have called his parents and they are on their way."

"Danny, they won't tell me anything. I don't know what's going on."

Danny hugged me. "They are doing surgery to repair

145

the torn artery in his neck and giving him blood. He lost a lot of blood. They won't know anything until he is out of surgery."

Donovan's parents arrived and Danny made the introductions, "Mrs. Sara, Mr. Donnie, this is Sherri and Constance."

Mrs. Sara leaned down and cupped Constance's face, "So this is my new granddaughter?"

Mr. Donnie poked her. "Oh, I'm sorry Sherri. I'm worried sick and I don't know what I'm saying. Donovan has told me all about y'all and how he thought of Constance as his daughter. I'm sorry."

She sat down in a chair. I walked over to her. "It's okay Mrs. Sara. Don't worry about it. I have said some things tonight that shocked me as well. He'll be okay. We just have to keep telling ourselves that."

We hugged. It seemed like a lifetime before the doctors came out. "Mr. and Mrs. Weston?"

They stood up. "That's us. How is our son?" asked Mr. Donnie.

The look on the doctor's face was grim. "We had to do surgery to repair a ruptured artery in his neck. We also had to repair a tear in his voice box. He had to have two and a half pints of blood. There was a loss of oxygen to his brain for a short time. We have him in a medically induced coma for at least the next several hours so he doesn't try to talk. He is stable at the moment but we won't know anything for sure until we can take him out of the coma. The good news is he still has brain activity so he is not brain dead but we can't tell you he is going to make a full recovery at this time."

"Can we see him?" I asked.

"Yes you can go in, but please one at a time."

I turned to Mrs. Sara, "Y'all please go first. I'm not leaving once I go in there, if that's okay with you."

146

"It's more than okay, Sherri. If he wakes up and doesn't see you there he would be heartbroken. He is crazy about you and this little family."

She went in for a few minutes and when she came out then Mr. Donnie went in. Danny offered to take Constance back to the hotel.

"Mom, I can't go back there. I want to stay here with you. I don't want to leave Donovan."

"Constance, Donovan won't be awake for a long time. You need to get some rest. Would you feel better if I called Steph and she could come take you to the hotel?"

Constance started crying. "I do NOT want to go back there. Anywhere but there, mom. I can't go back there. Someone might get me."

Mrs. Sara interrupted, "Constance, I have an idea. How about you come stay with us at our beach house while we wait on Donovan to wake up. I would love to get to know you and if anybody knows anything it will be us. We are his parents so they will let us know the minute anything happens. Would you like that?"

Constance looked up at me and I looked at Danny. "Constance, we will all be staying there so you won't be there by yourself," he assured her. Constance hesitantly agreed and they left for the night.

Sitting by his bedside I had plenty of time to think about what I told the cop. *Could it be true? It must be because it just came out of my mouth in the heat of the moment.*

I took Donovan's hand. "I don't know if you can hear me. The doctors seem to think you can, but I'm a little skeptical. I'm going to tell you this anyway and if you can hear me then you will know. I can't bear the thought of something happening to you and not telling you this. You helped us without strings and I can never thank you enough

147

for that. I don't know where I would be right now if it weren't for you. My daughter is happier than I ever could have imagined she could be without her daddy. Your mom told off on you," I said chuckling, "and just so you know, we are crazy about you too. As a matter of fact apparently without realizing it I have fallen in love with you. I didn't realize it until I told the officer tonight that you were the man I loved. This is not at all how I thought the conversation would ever go if I told another man I loved him."

His eyes fluttered and I ran into the hall shouting, "He is opening his eyes! Something is happening!"

The nurses came rushing in and checked his vitals and injected something into his I.V. "I thought he was in a coma," I said to the nurse.

"He is supposed to be but apparently he has a higher tolerance for medication than we thought. I sedated him. It's not good for him to come around and try to talk right now. It's just not safe."

I was hopeful yet heartbroken. It was a good sign that he was trying to wake up especially so soon but he needed to rest. I took his hand, "Donovan listen to me. I don't want anything to happen to you. They said you need your rest. I will be right here when you wake up and I will tell you again that I love you." I felt his finger stroke the palm of my hand once and then nothing.

I fell asleep in the chair next to his bed still holding his hand. The nurse came in and woke me up. "The couch folds out into a bed if you would be more comfortable there."

I shook my head, "No thank you. I need to be right here where I can hold his hand. I want him to know someone is here."

She smiled. "Well, if it would be more comfortable for you, you can get in the bed next to him as long as you don't pull out any wires or anything."

I jumped up. "Oh, that would be wonderful."

She helped me adjust his I.V. and wires so I could lie next to him without pulling anything out. I laid in the bed next to him and put my arm over his chest like I have done so many nights before. I finally drifted off to sleep.

I woke to Mrs. Sara's voice, "Sherri, its morning. Why don't you go back to the house and get a shower. I will stay with him for a while."

"Thank you, Mrs. Sara, but I can't leave his side. I won't until he wakes up."

She put her hand on my shoulder. "Sherri, you can call me mom. I know how Donovan feels about you and I consider you family. You have an amazing daughter and I would be proud to have y'all as family."

I smiled at her. "It's still a little early to call us family."

"It's never too early. Even if things with you and Donovan don't work out I will still consider you family."

I hugged her. "Thanks. You can never have enough family."

Danny arrived with Constance. "Has there been any change, mom?"

I told them about his eyes fluttering and how he ran his finger across my hand.

"That's a good thing, right?" Mrs. Sara asked.

"Well, the doctors said it was just a reflex and not to get overly excited about it, but I think he heard me talking to him to be honest. Has anyone heard anything about the guy that attacked him?"

"Yeah," Danny started, "the cops have been interrogating him all night, and they keep getting a different story every time. First he said he was jealous and figured if he got him out of the way you and Constance would be

149

with him. Then he said someone put him up to it but that story quickly changed to he just wanted the publicity that came from killing someone famous. They can't seem to get a straight story out of him."

I looked at Danny. "Do you really think Michael had anything to do with this?"

We exchanged knowing glances. "Well, Sherri," he said, "You know if he did that he is so full of himself he would have to gloat about it. Did he try to call you?"

I started digging in my purse looking for my cell phone. I finally found it. "I don't have any reception in here. I have a voicemail but I don't know who it's from. I will go outside and check it."

I went outside and dialed my voicemail and a familiar voice came on the other end. "I hope you're enjoying your new life. I'm sorry for everything that happened between us but you will come back to me. People always come groveling back to me. Until then, sweetheart."

If he had anything to do with Donovan's attack we wouldn't be able to prove it. He was very careful what he said on my voicemail. I am pretty sure it was him. Once Donovan gets better I will prove it if it's the last thing I do. I went back in and told Danny about the voicemail.

"He's slick, I'll give him that," Danny said.

"Look, all that matters right now is Donovan. I can't think about anything else but him right now. Do you mind taking care of Constance for a while? If you don't want to I can fly Steph out here and she can do it."

Danny looked at me crazy. "Are you serious? She is my favorite little girl besides y'all are family and family takes care of one another. I will take care of her as long as you need me to."

I started to go back into Donovan's room when the doctor came over. "The sedative should be wearing off soon. If you all want to go in there and wait for him to come around you can this one time. We aren't sure what kind of permanent damage has been done. He needs to be as quiet as possible for the next few days to give his voice box time to heal but we have put some paper and a pen in there for him to communicate."

We were all in his room talking. I was sitting on his bed holding his hand saying a silent prayer for him to come back to us. I turned my head to talk to Danny and I felt him snatch his hand away from me. I turned around and his eyes were open and he had a horrified look on his face.

I quickly got up and Mrs. Sara came running over. He was trying to talk but she put her finger over his mouth. "Sweetie, you can't talk right now. You are in the hospital." She handed him the paper and pen. "You can write what you need on here."

I went over to him. "I'm so glad your back. We were so worried about you."

He looked at his mom. *Who is this,* he wrote.

She looked at him puzzled. "You don't remember?"

He shook his head no.

"I'll go get the doctor," I told her.

"Well, Mr. Weston, it's nice to see those eyes again. We were worried about you. Are you in pain?" the doctor asked.

Donovan shook his head no and then wrote *What is going on with me? Why can't I talk? Why can't I remember?*

The doctor told him, "With the injury you have to your voice box we don't want you talking right now because you will strain your vocal cords and may not ever be able to talk right again. You were stabbed in the neck and lost a lot of blood. You had oxygen cut off to your brain for a short time so the memory loss is typical but not permanent."

151

The doctor continued by asking simple questions. How old he was. Where he was born. What year it is. Who each person in the room was. He knew everyone except Constance and me. I was heartbroken. I love him but I can't even tell him now because he doesn't even know who I am. The doctor explained that he has forgotten the past six months, but everything before that is very clear to him so his memory will come back it will just take time and patience, and then he left.

Donovan got his mom's attention. *Who is this?* He wrote and pointed at Constance and me. Mrs. Sara looked at Constance and me then back at him before she answered his question, "This is your girlfriend and her daughter."

He threw the paper and pen and motioned to the door. His mom quickly picked up the paper and pen. "What is it sweetie? Write it down."

He quickly scribbled on the paper *GET OUT!! Everyone but Danny! NOW!!*

We left the room. Constance was crying and I did my best to console her but I wanted to cry myself.

"He doesn't love me anymore. He doesn't even know who I am. Mom, he said he would never leave me but he did. He broke his promise."

I tried to explain to her what was going on when Mrs. Sara walked over to us. "Sherri, if you don't mind I would like to talk to her."

I don't know what she can do or say that I can't but it would take some stress off of me right now so I said it was okay. I watched as Mrs. Sara showed Constance pictures and could tell she was calming down. I was on the verge of a breakdown when Danny came out.

I ran to him. "What did he say?"

Danny looked at the floor. "He has a lot of questions. Will he ever be able to sing again? Exactly who were you to him? What you and Constance had to do with his life? Things like that. Then he wanted to speak to the doctor."

"So what happened?" I asked anxiously.

"I told him all I knew and he said he wanted to be alone after he talked to the doctor. He did ask me if you told him you loved him. I told him I didn't know."

So he did hear me, but he doesn't know who I am so it didn't mean anything to him.

Constance came over and hugged me. "Mom, he does care about us. It's not his fault he doesn't know who we are. Grandma Sara explained it all to me. She has pictures of me, you, and the boys that he sent her. That bad man took him away from us and now we have to get him back. We can't lose him, mom. I won't lose another daddy."

Why does she keep calling him daddy? She knew who her daddy was but this is the second time I have heard her refer to him as daddy. I shrugged it off. I can't worry about that right now.

"I know Constance. We will get him back, somehow."

The doctor came out and walked over to us. "He is very agitated right now. We had to sedate him again. I think it's best for him to stay sedated for a couple of days at least. He wants to know if he will ever sing again and I can't give him that answer right now. It's just too soon to tell. You can go in one at a time if you would like to see him before he goes back to sleep. Sherri, I suggest you and Constance wait until he is asleep. He gets really agitated when I bring you or your daughter up. You're welcome to go in after he goes to sleep though."

I just don't know how much more of this I can take. It's almost like he hates me when just the other day he was saying I was everything he wanted in life. If that was true how could he just forget me so easily?

I waited for everyone to leave to go back to the house before I went in his room. He may not remember me but I remembered him and I know I love him. I just hoped that would be enough to bring him back to us. I crawled in bed next to him, just like I did the night before, and tried to sleep but between the nightmares and the nurses coming in to check on him it was almost pointless.

The next morning Mrs. Sara insisted I go to her house and take a shower. I tried to argue but she was as insistent as her son.

I can't think of anything but Donovan. If Michael did this I will kill him myself. I decided to call him on the way back to the hospital. The phone was ringing and I thought to myself that I really didn't need to do this but before I could hang up Michael answered, "Well, hello sweetheart. I figured I would be hearing from you. Are you ready to come home where you belong?"

If I could reach through the phone I would strangle him, I swear it. "I will never come back to you no matter what you do. Did you have someone attack Donovan?"

He laughed. "Now why would I do that? I don't have to stoop to that level to get you back. Like I said before, you will come groveling back. They always do."

I lost my cool, "I don't know and don't care who they is, but I will never come back to you, groveling or otherwise. You're a sorry excuse of a man and I hate that I even have to share the same air you breathe. I swear you will pay for what you have done do Donovan!"

The bastard snickered. "You have to prove I did anything first. Love you sweetheart," he said and hung up.

I was boiling mad at this point and it's all I could do not to get on the first plane home and kill him, but my first priority has to be Donovan. Once he gets better I will see to it that Michael pays.

I had another sleepless night. I couldn't decide if

it's because of the anxiety of him being able to talk again or the nightmares. Regardless, I laid next to him in the bed.

Mrs. Sara came in early the next morning. "Constance wants to see you and the doctor said he will be waking up anytime now. Why don't you go see about your daughter and I will be here when he wakes up." I nodded and walked out of the room to find Constance.

She was sitting in the waiting area writing when I found her. "What are you working on?"

She smiled up at me. "It's a song for Donovan, mom. I really think he will like it."

I gave her a big hug and sat down trying not to look impatient although I don't think I succeeded. It seemed like hours passed before Mrs. Sara came out. "Danny, he wants to talk to you," she said as she walked over and sat next to Constance and me. "He still doesn't remember. His main concern right now is if he will ever be able to sing again. Singing has been his life since he was a child. I don't know what's going to happen if he can't sing anymore."

I put my hand on her shoulder trying to comfort her. "Let's not think about that. Let's keep positive thoughts that everything will be fine."

Danny came out. "Sherri, he wants to see you. Try not to push. He is still agitated and he doesn't need to get all worked up."

I slowly walked in the room. I stood close to the door and he stared at me like it was the first time he had ever seen me. I had no idea what to do or say. He sat up in the bed and winced because of the pain. I started to rush to him but had to stop myself. It's so hard not to touch him or tell him how I feel. He managed to sit up on his own and patted the bed next to him for me to sit. I walked to the end of the bed as far away from him as I could get and sat on the very edge. If I got too close I might touch him without thinking about what I was doing and I didn't want to freak him out, even though my heart was broken in about a million pieces at the moment.

He smiled and asked, "Are you always this hardheaded?" He patted the bed next to him. His voice sounded awful. I knew it had to be killing him inside but he didn't show it.

I stood up and walked to where I was instructed but stopped. "Look Donovan, I know you want me over there, but it's already killing me not to be able to touch you so maybe I should just stay over here."

I could see the hurt in his beautiful gray eyes as he asked, "You don't want to be near me? From what I understand we were inseparable."

I walked over to the bed and sat next to him. "We were. That's why I am having a hard time being around you and not touching you."

He took my face in his hands and stared deep in my eyes then his heart and oxygen monitors started going off.

CHAPTER 13

The nurses came rushing in and I jumped up to give them room. He looked at them and asked, "What's the problem?"

One nurse checked all his monitors and admitted, "Well, I don't know. Everything seems to be fine now, but it was almost like your heart stopped beating and you couldn't breathe, or according to these monitors anyway. Hmmm...I guess it was just a glitch in the monitors. You're feeling okay?"

He nodded. "As well as I can, I suppose." The nurses left and he turned to me, "Please sweetheart," - I cringed at that word and he caught me - "I'm sorry, did I say something wrong? Please come sit with me. We have a lot of catching up to do apparently."

I went and sat on the bed beside him. "Please don't call me sweetheart. I know you don't remember but trust me, you would never want to call me that."

He looked at me puzzled. "Well, please fill me in on what I don't remember because I would never want to say or do anything that would upset you."

"I don't think that's a good idea right now. You need your rest and don't need to get irritated and this will definitely irritate you."

He took my hand and begged, "Please. I need to know. I will promise to keep my cool. I need to know though. I want to remember you and you can help me do that."

The doctor came in and saved me. He talked to Donovan about how he was feeling and told him he was improving remarkably. They still aren't sure if he will be able to sing again, and only time will tell, but he will be able to go home soon. The doctor left.

Donovan looked at me. "Home? Do I still have my

157

house or do we live together?"

I started to laugh. "Well, you still have your house, but you haven't been there in a while."

He looked at me quizzically, "I guess that goes back to what's happened that I can't remember. You were about to tell me when the doctor came in."

"I really don't…" I was trying to get out of telling him when Constance burst in.

"Donovan!!! I know you don't know who I am but I am going to help you remember me. That bad man isn't going to keep you away from me."

"Well, I may not remember you but you sure are cute. Mommy, why don't you put her up here to sit with me so we can talk?"

I sat Constance on the bed and she started to tell Donovan all about him and her. She ended with telling him about the pinky promise he made to her. "Well, I don't make promises I can't keep, especially pinky promises. So I'm going to make you another promise right now. I pinky promise that I will remember you and it will be like nothing ever happened. You sound like a special little girl and I want to remember that."

They did their pinky shake to seal the deal. "I just wish I could remember. It's killing me not to."

Constance looked at him and said, "I have something that might help." She ran out of the room and came back a few seconds later with her guitar. "Maybe this will help you remember." She started to play and sing one of the duets they had performed many times together and at the end of the last concert they played. She got to the part where Donovan was supposed to sing and stopped. "That was your part. Let me start over. I can sing your part too but I was hoping you would remember." She started again. She got to Donovan's part and after a couple of words he started to sing with her. His voice sounded horrible and he stopped. She stopped playing and went over to him, "See, you do remember!"

He had a look of horror on his face, "Please everybody get out but Sherri!"

Constance was very upset and looked at me. "I'm sorry, mom. I thought it would help him. I didn't want to hurt him." She ran out of the room crying.

I sat on the bed next to him. "What's wrong? What do you remember?"

He looked at me and his eyes were filled with tears. "I remember the concert. We sang that song. I remember introducing you to the crowd as my girlfriend and I remember being at the party when…" his voice trailed off.

I took his hand. "Donovan, I know it's hard but I need you to try to remember."

He looked at me. "I remember taking a picture and then being stabbed. That's all I remember. Why would someone want to stab me? Who is he? Did they catch him?"

I took a deep breath. "Slow down. I'm going to get them to give you something to calm your nerves and then I will tell you everything you want to know if the doctor says it's okay."

The nurse came in and gave him something to calm him down before he left again.

"So are you going to tell me now? I think I deserve to know how I ended up almost dying and why my singing career is in jeopardy."

I walked over, took his hand, and told him all about everything that had happened with Michael. "That doesn't tell me why I was so worried about you and how we ended up together," he commented.

I wanted him to remember that on his own, but I could see he wasn't going to let it go. "I only know what

159

you told me about that and what happened after we got together."

He looked at me waiting for me to elaborate. "You said there was a video of Constance that your girlfriend at the time told you about." I started laughing, "Then you tried to tell me that when you watched it the first time all you saw was me. You said that your heart stopped beating and you couldn't breathe."

He took my hand. "Well, that explains it."

I look at him puzzled. "Explains what?"

He smiled. "The monitors." I just looked at him not knowing what he was talking about until he explained, "When I looked into your eyes it was like seeing you for the first time. The heart and oxygen monitor didn't have a glitch, my heart literally stopped and I couldn't breathe. I thought it was something to do with my injury but I didn't want to worry anyone so I didn't say anything. It makes so much sense to me now." I could see in his eyes that he was serious. "Sherri, I don't remember us but I feel that you meant so much to me. From everything that Danny has told me I'm in love with you. Did I ever tell you that I loved you?"

I was stunned to hear him say that. I wanted to tell him I loved him too but I didn't feel now would be the right time. "No, you never did. Is that really how you feel?"

He chuckled. "I would love to be able to tell you it is but honestly I don't remember. I know that nobody has ever made my heart stop like that so that has to mean something, right?"

I felt utterly devastated. "I'm not sure what that means."

"Well, apparently you care a lot about me because my mom and Danny said you have been here since the attack and have even slept next to me. Was that you telling me you loved me while I was asleep?"

160

I didn't want to tell him the truth. I wanted to wait until all of this was behind us. "No, it must have been Constance. She loves you to death and this really scared her." I hated to lie to him but it's just too soon for me to tell him how I feel, especially for the first time.

"So, this guy that attacked me. Do you really think Michael had anything to do with it?"

I told him about the phone calls with Michael and that we didn't have any proof but I was pretty sure he was.

"I wouldn't put it past him with all the stuff he has apparently put us through. I just can't believe he would do something like this. I'm sorry I upset Constance. Can you get her back in here for me?"

Constance came back in and I put her back on the bed next to him. "Constance, your mom has told me all about everything that I can't remember and it sounds like you have had a pretty rough time of it. I just wish there was some way I could make it all up to you."

I have never been more proud of my little girl when she turned to him and said, "I just want you to get better and come back to us. We miss you, don't we, mommy?"

I nodded my head.

"Wait," he said, "What about the tour?"

"Danny said it was our last stop."

"What about my fans? I can't let them down."

"Donovan, they understand. They just want you to get better. That's what we all want."

The doctor came back in. "Okay, visiting hours are just about over. I do have good news though. I think it would be easier for you to rest and get better at home. You're stable and all your vital signs are looking good so I think we will let you go home in the morning, if you want."

Donovan looked at the doctor crazy. "If I want? Of course I want to go home. I have to get my life back and I can't do it sitting in this hospital bed."

The doctor gave us a few more minutes and then everyone had to leave. I walked over and kissed Donovan on the forehead. As we were leaving Donovan asked, "Sherri, will you stay with me please?"

If he had his memory he would know that I wouldn't say no to him right now. "Of course, I will."

I sat in the chair and everyone else went home.

He laughed. "Now that I'm conscious you don't want to be near me?"

I got up and moved toward the bed. "I'm sorry. I just didn't want to freak you out."

He pulled me on the bed. "I'm sorry I reacted like that when I woke up, but I didn't know what was going on. Just because my memory is gone doesn't mean I don't want to be with you. I may not remember us but I know what you mean to me. I wouldn't have done all of the things you say I did if you didn't mean the world to me. Lay down with me, please."

I lay in the bed with him the same way I had the previous nights but this time he wrapped his arms around me and I slept like a baby.

A kiss on my forehead woke me up. "Good morning, babe. I hope you slept well."

He called me babe. Did he get his memory back already?

"Good morning. I did sleep pretty well. You called me babe. Is your memory back?"

He squeezed me tight, "Not yet, but I did have what seemed like a dream last night. It was a lot like what you told me about you and me yesterday. I still can't remember much of the Michael drama other than the whole video incident but maybe it's starting to come back."

I sat up in the bed. "When you get out of here today where do you want to go? I think it might be best if you go to your mom's for a little while."

He gently stroked my hair. "Only if you'll go with me and promise not to leave me there by myself."

I chuckled. "You'll have to beat me to get me to go away."

"Oh, so you like it rough, huh babe?"

There is so much of him in there I can see that the Donovan I have grown to love is the real Donovan which makes me love him even more. I never thought it would be possible to love anyone after Jonathan but I can see that I was so wrong. I decided I was going to tell him. He may not remember me, but he seemed to know how he felt about me so he needed to know how I felt about him.

"Donovan, I need to tell you something. I lied to you before when I said –"

Constance came running in the door followed by Sara and Donnie. "Are you ready to go? It's been lonely at the house without you," she said climbing on a chair to get close to him. She kissed him on the nose and he tickled her.

"You bet I am, sweet pea, but where am I going to go?"

He looked at me with a knowing glance. She jumped up and down. "MOM, he called me sweet pea!! Did you hear that? He's in there, I just know it!" Once she calmed down she continued, "Grandma Sara's, silly. Where else would you go?"

He hugged her. "Well, only if you and your mommy are going to be there."

The doctor made him an appointment to come back and see about his wound, told him to take it easy and no singing, and released him.

We all went to his parent's beach house. "Sherri, do you think Steph and the boys would want to come out and stay a little while?" Mrs. Sara asked. "I'm sure they are

163

tired of sitting around that house."

"Thank you Mrs. Sara –"

She interrupted, "Please just call me mom. It would make me feel a lot better."

"Okay, thanks mom, but I don't want to have too many people in this house. Donovan needs his rest and he won't get it with all the kids here."

Donovan spoke up, "Excuse me babe, but I would rather have the whole family here. I know you miss them and it would take some stress off of you. Please bring them out."

I called Steph only to find out she was very upset with me because she had been trying to get in touch with me since all of this started. "I'm sorry, Steph. I had no service in the hospital and I wasn't leaving his side. I promise I won't do it again." We set everything up and said goodbye.

"She and the kids will be here tomorrow at 4:15 p.m.," I told them.

"We will pick them up at the airport," Mrs. Sara said.

Donovan stood up and put his arm around his mom's shoulders, "Mom, stop trying so hard. Just be yourself and I'm sure they are going to love you, besides Sherri, Constance, and I will be picking them up. They don't know you and I think everybody has been through enough the last couple of months. We just all need some family time and everything will be fine."

She looked hurt and changed the subject. "So, what does my boy want for dinner tonight? I know you remember how much you love your mama's cooking."

He leaned over and whispered something in Mrs. Sara's ear and she turned to me. "How would you feel about cooking tonight? With my help, of course."

I was stunned at the request. What did he say to

her? Oh well, doesn't matter.

"I would love to, but when it comes to cooking I'm quite anal."

She laughed. "Reminds me of someone else I know," she said as she kissed Donovan on the cheek. "Let's go get started."

When we were done eating Mrs. Sara looked at Donovan. "It looks like you were right, son."

I looked at them smiling. "What was he right about?"

Sara started to speak but Donovan stopped her, "Well, I wasn't sure so I didn't say anything in front of you because I didn't want to get your hopes up, but when mom mentioned eating, something told me I wanted to eat your cooking and boy was I right!"

I was so happy. His memory is coming back in pieces, but it's coming back and that's all that matters.

Constance was on the couch with Sara and Donnie watching television and Donovan took my hand and asked, "Will you walk on the beach with me? I would really like some time alone with you." That sounded like the best idea I had heard in a while.

We walked out on the beach hand in hand. "Sherri, I don't know what's going on with me. I may not remember us, but I just have this feeling that I always want to be close to you and touching you even if it's only in the smallest way. My mind may not be all here, but my body is telling me everything I need to know."

We walked for a while in silence until he stopped and turned to me, "You were going to tell me something in the hospital. Something about a lie you told me?"

I was hoping he had forgotten all about that. He took my face in his hands, "Sherri, I have a confession also.

165

I may not remember everything I need to remember, but I do know one thing…I love you."

I pulled away from him and ran off down the beach crying. How could he tell me this right now? He doesn't even know me anymore but he is claiming to love me. I sat down in the sand and put my head in my hands and cried.

Donovan caught up to me and sat beside me. "Sherri, I'm so sorry. I didn't want to upset you but I don't want to let another day go by without telling you." Silence. He put his arm around me. "Sherri, please say something to me."

I turned to him, "Donovan, how can you tell me you love me? You don't even know me, but I do know you and I do love you and I didn't want to tell you like this. The lie I told was that it was me that told you I loved you at the hospital. I wanted to wait until you got your memory back to tell you."

I could see how hurt he was. "Sherri, how can you tell me I don't know how I feel? How much more proof do you need? When I saw you for the first time my heart stopped and I couldn't breathe. When I looked into your eyes in the hospital and it was like seeing you for the first time again and the same thing happened. I don't remember your cooking, but apparently somewhere deep inside me I knew that you were an awesome cook. I don't have to remember us to know how I feel about you."

He lifted my head so that our eyes met and kissed me in a way that sent chills all over my body. He has never kissed me like that before. He stopped and looked at me. "Sherri, I honestly, truly love you."

He didn't lie about the first time he saw me. There was something about that kiss and then looking into his eyes. Why I believed him I wasn't sure but I did.

"Donovan, I believe you. I love you too."

We made love on the sand under the stars. It was

much more passionate than the time before. There was a connection there that neither of us could deny. We sat up sweating and breathless.

"I'm so sorry that I didn't believe you, Donovan, but you have to understand my doubt. Well, I guess you don't but if you had your memory you would."

He looked at me. "It's Michael, isn't it? What did he do to you? What are you not telling me?" I told him all the parts of Michael and I that I had left out. His jaw was in the sand when he finally said, "I can't believe he did that to you. I'm so sorry. I would do anything to go back and change things. Did I try to stop him at all? How could I have let him do that to you?"

"No, Donovan, don't blame yourself. You really tried but I was so wrapped up in Michael and listened to him instead of letting you have your say that I turned you away more than once. You did everything you could."

"I'm still confused about it all. I can see now why I beat him up, but how did I end up getting arrested and what is going on with the trial? All this is happening and the only thing I know for sure is that I love you, Constance, and the boys. Everything else is like a jumbled puzzle in my head. You keep giving me bits and pieces but it's confusing me."

I pushed him down in the sand, kissed him, and then lay next to him. "I will start from the beginning. If you don't understand something just stop me and let me know."

I started with telling him about Jonathan. "I'm so sorry babe," he said. "Sounds like you had it rough before you ever got here."

I put my finger over his mouth. "If you want this to make sense let me finish telling you everything or I will get lost and leave stuff out. Then you can ask questions about what you don't understand."

He laughed at me. "Are you always this bossy?"

I continued telling him the whole story from start to

167

finish. When I was done he looked at me in amazement. "I can't believe you have been through all of that. I can't believe you thought I would want to harm you, although I can see why. Michael is a terrible person. I never thought he was capable of this. Now I know that I was right all along."

I looked at him puzzled. "About what?" I asked.

He smiled, leaned over, and kissed me on the nose. "That I love you. You are such an incredible woman. I want our life back. I don't care if my memory comes back, I have all I need right here and I know everything I need to know about you."

"But Donovan, you have to get your memory back or Michael might get away with this all."

He brushed my hair out of my face. "I won't ever let that happen. He will never hurt you or my family again," he promised.

His family? What had Michael done to his family?

He could see me thinking. "Sherri, I mean you, me, and your kids. You're my family now. Grandma Sara said so," he clarified and started laughing.

Constance hollered out the door looking for us so we went back to the house.

We went to the airport to pick up Steph and the boys. They came running out of the airport hollering and running for Donovan. Constance stepped in front of them, "STOP! Donovan doesn't know who you are so you have to go easy on him. Some bad man stabbed him and his memory fell out."

We all laughed. Donovan went over to the boys and picked them both up. "I remember you two," he said. To Drew, "You can sing really well," and Charlie, "And you, my good man, love your mama." He hugged them both. Constance and I were both staring at him scared to say

168

anything. I didn't want to get my hopes up yet again.

"Donovan, you remember them?" I asked hoping for him to say yes.

He put the boys down. "After our talk last night when you told me everything I have been having flashes of what I guess is my memory. I was going to surprise you when I got it all back, but I can't have these boys thinking I don't know who they are."

"So what are you remembering?" I asked.

"Well it's all still a little fuzzy but I remember running into y'all at the studio and that's where Charlie here wanted to make sure I knew that you were with Michael. I remember coming to your house and hearing Drew sing. I remember a dinner that you and I had –"

I started blushing. "Yeah, I think we need to talk about this later when little ears aren't around."

Steph started laughing. "Yeah, and me too."

CHAPTER 14

We got to the house and I was about to tell everyone about Donovan's breakthrough but he stopped me. "Let's wait until I'm one hundred percent before we say anything. We still don't know what's going to happen with my voice."

I hugged him. "Donovan, everything is going to be just fine. I have faith."

Mrs. Sara came over to us. "Donovan, the police called. They need you and Sherri to come down and do a lineup. They know they have the guy but said this was merely a formality. Do you feel up to it?"

He hugged her. "Mom, I need to do this. I want this guy to pay and I want to make sure this never happens to anyone else. We'll go now to get it over with."

She smiled at me. "Why don't the two of you take the night to yourselves? I took the liberty of renting you a room so you could have some alone time."

He gave her a look. "Mom, you shouldn't have done that without asking me first. What I need right now is to spend time with my family. We haven't seen the boys in a while and they need to be with their mother."

I took his hand to calm him down. "Thank you, mom," I said, "but we would rather be here with the boys if it's not too much trouble. Donovan knows how much I love my kids and knows I wouldn't want to be anywhere else." She turned and walked away.

"I hope I didn't make her mad," I said.

He kissed me on the nose. "It doesn't matter if you did. All that matters is what we want, not what everybody else wants for us. We will get through this together and if she doesn't like that then I'm sorry for her."

I've never heard him talk about his mom like that. It's good that he isn't a mama's boy but I'm not sure I like him treating her like that.

We walked into the police station and everybody stopped what they were doing and started staring at us. An officer came over, introduced himself, and led us to a private room. We all sat down and the officer started the conversation, "We have been talking to this guy since we brought him in. He has said more than once he wasn't acting alone but when we press for more information he changes his story. Do you have any idea who he could have been working with?"

Donovan looked at me so I answered, "Well, officer, if you want my honest opinion it was Michael Stargate."

The officer looked at me crazy, "As in the actor and singer?" He shook his head disbelievingly and continued, "Well, I guess anything is possible in this day and age. We'll look into it and see what we can find. We'll need you here for trial but other than that we can do everything over the phone."

Another officer knocked on the door to let us know they were ready for us to view the lineup. They let us go in together but Donovan had to be the first to make the identification. We stood there holding hands as they brought the suspects in. When he saw the guy who stabbed him he squeezed my hand so hard it hurt. We made the identification and left after Donovan gave out several autographs.

Needless to say the ride back to the house was silent and he seemed rather distant.

When I woke up the next morning Donovan wasn't there. I couldn't find him anywhere in the house but Mrs. Sara was in the kitchen. "Mrs. Sara, I'm sorry, mom, have you seen Donovan?"

She handed me a cup of juice. "He's probably in his special place. When he was little and he got upset he would go to his special place and write. There is a large cliff that overlooks the ocean down the beach a ways. You'll probably find him there."

I walked down the beach and the cliffs came into my view. It wasn't far from the house but far enough someone could be alone if they wanted to. I saw him sitting on the cliff the same way I had seen him that morning sitting on the beach, no shirt on and hair flying in the wind. He sat with his legs dangling over the edge looking out over the ocean.

I slowly walked up behind him and put my hand on his shoulder. He jumped like I scared him to death. "Sherri, how did you find me?"

"Your mom told me where you would probably be. Are you okay? You haven't had much to say since last night."

He hung his head down. "Sherri, when I woke up this morning my first thought was revenge on Michael. I was going to fly home and hurt him the way he hurt the both of us but then I rolled over and saw your beautiful face and I realized I couldn't do that after everything you did to keep me from killing him before and I have just felt ashamed all day."

"Donovan, I never told you about that. I never told you about keeping you at my house so that you didn't do anything stupid. Are you getting more of your memory back?"

He looked up at me. "When I woke up this morning and remembered that, it was like a tidal wave of memories. I remember it all now." He looked hurt. "How could I have ever forgotten you? How could I have put you through so much and forgotten what you mean to me?"

I sat next to him and gently turned his head so that

he was looking at me. "Donovan, it's okay. It worked itself out and we're fine. You didn't do anything to me."

His eyes filled with tears. "Yes I did, Sherri. I didn't remember the woman of my dreams. The woman I love with all of my heart. I can't begin to imagine how hurt you must have been. I'm so sorry babe, so, so sorry."

I put my arms around him. "No, Donovan. It wasn't your fault and I know that. There was nothing you could've done."

He pulled away from me. "Yes, there was. I should have known. If I loved you enough I would have known no matter how my memory was."

I looked at him. "Look me in the eyes and listen to me. There was nothing you could have done. I don't doubt how much you love me and I never will. We will get through this together. I love you so much and I just want you to know that I will never hold that against you. It was a reflex, that's all."

The tears spilled over and rolled down his cheeks. "I just feel so horrible."

I kissed him passionately and said, "Well, don't. I love you and you love me and that's all that matters." The look he gave me told me he still wasn't convinced. Donovan, I love you and you're not going to lose me over something like that."

He turned away from me. "No, but what if I can't sing again. You will leave me for sure then."

I let out an exasperated sigh, disgusted by what he had said. "I can't believe you. You have your memory back so you should know better than that. I don't think any of this is what is really bothering you. I think you are scared that your singing career is over and that's the problem."

He turned back to me. "I guess you're probably right. Listen to my voice, it sounds horrible. All I have ever wanted to do was sing. If I lose that I will have nothing."

"You're wrong, Donovan. You will still have us and you have already had a successful career, which is more than most people. You should be counting your blessings. You could have died in that operating room."

I got up and walked off so hurt and irritated. *I can't believe he would even THINK I would leave if he couldn't sing again. How could he not be happy to be alive?* I made it halfway back to the house before he caught up to me. "Sherri, I'm sorry, again. I hate to admit it but I'm an emotional wreck right now."

"I know and understand that, but I just don't know how to get through to you that we aren't going anywhere and everything will work itself out, one way or the other. Whatever happens, we'll get through it. As long as we are together we can take on the world."

"You're such an amazing person and I'm so lucky to have you in my life. I don't know how I would get through all of this without you."

"Donovan, you probably wouldn't be in this mess if it weren't for me."

He took my hand and we walked toward the house. "It probably would have happened eventually anyway. Michael has been out for me since the first day he laid eyes on me."

As we walked in the house Mrs. Sara came running, phone in hand. "Donovan, the police station just called. They have news and need you to call them immediately."

He took the phone from her and called the precinct. We all stood there anxiously waiting for him to finish the call and tell us what was going on. He talked for a few minutes then hung up the phone and said, "Well, they think they have found the connection between this guy and Michael. They are picking Michael up for questioning and revoking his bail. He wouldn't tell me what they found but if they are revoking his bail it must be pretty incriminating, right?" He hugged me. "I'm so antsy right now. I can't just sit here. I think we should pack up and head home. Maybe there I can get back in the studio."

I backed away from him. "But, Donovan, you can't sing right now."

He laughed. "No, I meant to write. Not to mention we have a meeting with the label for Constance. Well, you do anyway. My career may be on hold but there is no reason hers has to be."

Mrs. Sara objected, "But, Donovan, you have to see the doctor in a week. Don't you think you should stay at least until then?"

He hugged her. "Can't, mom, too much to do," he said as he put his plan into motion.

It didn't take long at all to pack and get loaded into the car. Donovan had a jet waiting for us at the airport and Mrs. Sara dropped us off. As we were getting out she addressed me, "Sherri, would you like the boys to stay here with me until y'all come back next week? I would love to spend some time with them."

Donovan threw a fit. "No, mom! Sherri hasn't been able to see her kids in a while and they are coming home with us."

I stepped in, "Donovan, that will be fine. We don't know what will be waiting for us when we get home and I'm sure Steph could use a break."

Donovan looked at the boys. "I guess it's up to them then." Of course, the boys wanted to stay.

It was so nice to be home again. There was so much to do to get back in the swing of things. There was only a week left until I started catering my first party. First things first, Donovan called Mr. James to see what was going on.

"Mr. James said he needs us in his office first thing

in the morning to meet with the record label. We will have Mr. Johnson meet us there so you can sign all the contracts. Then they want her in the studio tomorrow after we sign the papers. Are you ready for all of this?"

I laughed. "It doesn't look like I have much choice, now do I?"

The next morning we signed the papers and headed to the studio. Donovan walked Constance through everything. "Donovan, will you sit with me while I sing?" she asked.

I could see the hurt in his eyes. "Sweet pea, I can't sing right now."

She smiled at him. "I know silly but you can sit in the room with me while I sing, can't you?"

His hurt turned to joy. "Sure I can. Let's go."

She started to sing a song that was written for her but stopped. "I'm not singing this. I only want to sing songs that either I or Donovan wrote."

Donovan tried to explain to her that she had to sing whatever they told her to but she wasn't hearing it. She ran out of the studio crying with Donovan close behind her. I went out behind them only to hear Donovan trying to fix the situation. "Sweet pea, if you don't want to sing the songs they give you then you will break your contract. You need to make sure that's what you want to do because if you do I will fix this."

I said, "Donovan, I'm not going to let you do that. That will take a lot of money and I won't hear of it. You have done so much for us but I'm not letting you do this." I turned to Constance. "Darling, you have to do what they tell you. You can't just do what you want anymore. You're the star but they are your bosses so you have to listen to them."

"But mom, I really don't want to sing those songs.

They aren't me. I like the songs that Donovan and I wrote," she said.

I hugged her. "I'm sorry, Constance, but you signed a contract, and that's what the contract says."

Just then one of the executives walked out. "Donovan, as her manager we need to talk."

Donovan straightened him out quickly. "I'm not her manager. Her mom is."

I followed the executive inside, as did Donovan with Constance in tow.

"Look Sherri," the exec said, "we don't normally do this, but we have talked about it and decided it's okay if she only wants to do hers or Donovan's songs. Donovan has been writing songs as long as I can remember and not one of them has ever bombed, so if that's what she wants then we will be happy with that." He turned to Constance, "But young lady, we pick the songs." The smile immediately came back to her face as she nodded with excitement.

The three of us were in the studio the rest of the week. Constance got her first hit album done and then it was time to go back to Seattle for Donovan's doctor's appointment. We flew in on Sunday to spend the night with his parents and from there to the doctor the next morning. I wasn't sure who was more nervous, him or me.

We took a seat in the waiting room. Finally the nurse called him back. He grabbed my hand to let me know I was going with him. We sat in the room in complete silence waiting. When the doctor came in I went and sat next to Donovan and held his hand. The exam only took a few minutes and the doctor pulled up a chair and took a seat to explain everything to us.

"Well, Donovan," he began, "everything is healing quite well. Unfortunately, your voice isn't returning to normal. I'm so sorry to have to tell you this but it doesn't look like you will be returning to singing any time soon, if ever. We need to see you back in a year and we will check your progress then." The doctor told Donovan again how sorry he was that he didn't have better news for us and wished him well as he departed the exam room.

Donovan broke down and started crying as soon as the doctor closed the door behind him. I didn't know what to say. This must be so hard for him. If only there was something I could do to make it all better.

We got back to his parent's house to find that his mom had put together a small party to celebrate only she didn't know the news was bad. Donovan saw the balloons, cake, and streamers and ran out the back door. I explained to Mrs. Sara very hurriedly everything the doctor had said and ran out the door after him. He was nowhere in sight but I knew where to look for him.

I found him on the cliff. I walked up and sat next to him. "Donovan, it's not the end of the world. You have had a great career and who knows, maybe in a year you will be back on the road. Until then you still have your writing and you could possibly do some more acting." We sat in silence staring out over the ocean for what seemed like hours. I tried again, "Donovan, you have to know I still love you no matter what."

He put his head on my shoulder. "Even if I'm washed up and unemployed?" he asked.

I laughed. "Donovan, you're not unemployed and we don't know that you're washed up...Wait that came out wrong. What I meant was you're not washed up. You have your whole life in front of you. Why can't you see that? You're so lucky to still be alive. I guess maybe I just have a different view than you do but you almost died on the operating table. I almost lost you before I could even tell you I loved you!" The tears flowed rapidly down my cheeks as I continued, "I can't lose another person I love to something stupid. I just can't!"

He hugged me. "I'm trying to see it from your perspective but all I can see is that I have lost the one thing in my life that I thought I could always depend on. No matter what happened in my life I thought it would never let me down. I have been doing it so long I don't know if I can do without it."

I looked at him and told him honestly, "I'm that rock now. I will never let you down. You can always depend on me to be there. I keep saying this, but we will get through this together and I mean it. I am not going anywhere unless you chose for me to go." I smiled at him and held my pinky finger out, "Pinky promise."

After our talk we walked back to the house and as we went inside Mrs. Sara came over to him and took his hands in hers. "I'm so sorry son. I really thought that everything would be fine."

He hugged her. "It's okay, mom. I'm really blessed. We will get through this, or so I keep being told, but in the meantime we do have something to celebrate."

He turned to everyone. "We may not be celebrating me, but we have something even more amazing to celebrate. Everyone say congratulations on her first big record deal to Constance."

The party was great but I could tell he wasn't really into it. Once everything winded down we headed to the airport. Since I had a party to do the next day I had a ton of things to start getting ready.

As we got off the plane it was evident that someone had already leaked the news and the paparazzi were waiting for us. Constance took front and center to get us through it. She drew their attention while I got Donovan in the car.

Once we turned on our street it was evident that the paparazzi nightmare wasn't just at the airport. We couldn't get down the street because of all the people there.

I turned to Donovan. "What do you want to do? We can't go on like this and they aren't going to stop until they get what they want, you know that."

He put his head in his hands. "I'll handle it. You and Constance stay in the car until I tell you to get out." He took a deep breath and opened the door.

"Look, I know y'all want a statement and I will give you one, on one condition. You all have to leave and agree to leave us alone. We just want to live our lives in peace," Donovan told the crowd. They all looked at each other then back at him and nodded as if accepting his condition. He continued, "I have not been cleared to sing again. I'm not sure when or if I will but when I do I will let you guys know. I have other business ventures in the works but can't tell you about them at this moment until something is final. Sherri and I are still together and plan to stay that way so I would appreciate it if you could give us some space. You should also know that Sherri has started her own catering business and if you have never had her cooking I suggest you book a party because you won't be disappointed. The police have picked up Michael as the mastermind behind the attack and we will be going to trial soon. I am lucky to be alive so please leave me alone and let me live my life. Thank you."

He stood there as different ones started shouting questions. Calmly he replied, "I have said all I'm going to say. Now, please leave." They stood there astonished before they slowly started trickling back to their vehicles.

He opened the door for us to get out. "Donovan, what business ventures were you referring to? I didn't know anything about any of this," I asked curiously.

He smiled at me. "It's what they wanted to hear so I

told them that to get them to go away. But I have to help
Constance with her writing and you with your catering so I
have a lot on my plate, even with my career being on hold."

CHAPTER 15

This party was going to be our first public outing since the accident and also since Donovan announced to everyone that we were dating though I'm not so sure it's a good idea for him to go. "Donovan, if you want to skip the party tomorrow I will completely understand. It's going to be a bit much, I think."

He wrapped his arms around me. "Babe, there is no way I'm sending you out there alone. It's going to be hectic and you shouldn't have to deal with it all on your own. Besides, it will do me good to get out and mingle I think."

I was so busy running around finishing up last minute details but I noticed that he wasn't the same happy-go-lucky guy I have come to know. He is really taking this hard. I guess I can understand but there has to be a way to get him out of this funk. The party was great. Nobody mentioned the accident, instead they were all interested in the food and Donovan and I being a couple. Every time someone mentioned me his face lit up but I could still see the disheartenment in his stance.

At home lying in bed with Donovan I mentioned, "I have two more parties this week, Michael's trial begins, and Constance is needed in the studio. I don't know how I'm going to handle it all."

He pulled me to him. "I'm here. You don't have to do this all yourself. I can take care of Constance and the studio and help you with the cooking. The trial will take the both of us so there is no way I can get you out of that but we will get through it together. Isn't that what you keep telling me?"

I didn't see much of Donovan or Constance the next

few days but things seem to be working themselves out. What I did see was Donovan keeping busy and not having time to worry about his career, or so I thought. Lying in bed the night before Michael's trial I had a million things running through my head but my heart plummeted when Donovan turned to me and said, "Sherri, we need to talk."

That's never a good thing. Breathe Sherri. "Should I be worried?" I asked.

He started laughing. "Well, I hope not. The thing is I'm always here and I have a perfectly good house that is just sitting empty."

"I don't understand, Donovan. Are you asking me to move in with you?"

He shrugged his shoulders. "Would it be such a bad thing?"

Apparently I took too much time thinking about it because he said, "Okay, I can see you're hesitant, but what would be the problem?"

I had to think about how to respond so as not to hurt his feelings again. "Well, this is the only thing we have been able to call ours since Jonathan died. The kids need stability and since we've gotten here I haven't really been able to give it to them."

I could see the wheels turning in his head. "I can understand that. How about we don't move in my house, but we sell both houses and buy one for all of us. Yours is so small and mine is too big. We could find one that would suit all of us. Besides, I don't need that house really. It was always too big but when I started making money I thought I needed to spend it all before it ran out," he said laughing.

"Donovan, I just don't know. I can't just uproot the kids yet again. I haven't even seen much of the boys since Constance started her tour and I don't know if I can ask this of them. At least not now."

He is determined though. "Well, how about we put

it to a vote in the morning at breakfast."

I chuckled. "You're not going to give this up are you?"

"Sherri, I just really want to start our lives and I feel like getting a place together would be a great start."

I finally gave in to a vote at breakfast. "If and only if the boys seem excited about it will we do it."

We all sat at the table eating breakfast as I contemplated how to approach the subject but Donovan beat me to it. "So, kids, your mom and I were talking last night and we need your opinion on something. What would y'all think about moving in together, all of us?"

Drew laughed. "We do live together silly. You're always here."

Donovan laughed as well. "No, I mean buy a house where we can all live."

Charlie thought it over and asked, "What about Steph?"

Donovan patted Steph on the shoulder. "Well, Steph is part of this family so of course she would move in with us. If she wanted to that is."

All three kids went wild with excitement. After a few seconds of nonstop chatter and enthusiasm Constance went still. "Do we get to help pick it out?" she asked intriguingly.

"Well of course you do," Donovan told her.

"Then let's do it!" she hollered.

"Okay, well we have a lot to do the next couple of days, but this weekend we will start looking. Deal?"

"YEAH!!" they screamed in unison.

We headed to the courthouse for the first day of Michael's trial. Everyone was sitting waiting for court to start. Michael was with his lawyer but kept giving us dirty looks. The Judge came in to start court and after court was brought into session the prosecution's lawyer addressed the court. "Your honor, we are upgrading the charges to include attempted murder."

Michael's lawyer objected, "On what grounds?"

They give Michael's lawyer the paperwork. He looked at it then looked at Michael, who had buried his head in his hands. Michael's lawyer requested a recess to look over the new material and talk with his client. The Judge obliged and court was adjourned for the day.

As we walked out of the courtroom Donovan turned to me, "Since we took the whole day off for court, why don't we go do something just the two of us?"

I was intrigued. "What exactly did you have in mind?"

He smiled. "I'll show you. Come on."

He drove us toward the beach. The houses there were absolutely gorgeous. He pulled in a driveway with a "FOR SALE" sign in the front yard. "Donovan, what did you do?"

He laughed. "You know me all too well but I didn't do anything. I just wanted to see what you thought of this house is all."

I looked at him doubtful. "So, you didn't buy it?"

He hugged me. "No babe. Believe it or not I really didn't. I did put my house on the market though and already have a buyer so we need to get on the ball."

He punched in the code on the door lock and we went in. To say it was beautiful would be injustice. We looked at room after room. The master bedroom looked out over the ocean with a big bay window so we could watch the sunset over the ocean. We rushed through the rooms and it seemed he was hurrying me through the house for some reason.

"Finally the last room, the kitchen. Don't you love

it, Sherri? Look at all the room you have in here. Look at this refrigerator and this stove. You could cook for an army on this stove."

Of course, he is right. It's perfect for us. "We have to get the kids first. They have the final say so."

He kissed me in the foyer underneath the crystal chandelier. I called Steph and gave her the address and asked her to meet us with the kids. I could hear them all when they get out of the car. By the sounds of the squeals they approve.

We gave them the grand tour and Charlie was the first to speak up. "When can we move in mom?"

Donovan and I looked at each other. "Charlie, we weren't sure y'all would like it but if you do we will see how soon we can get it."

They all three screamed with excitement. We already had so much to do and now we were adding moving to the mix. I actually missed my old boring life.

Mr. Johnson called. "Donovan, they want to offer him a plea deal. You have to approve it first. As your lawyer I'm advising you to turn it down but I'm sure you will anyway. They are offering a plea of guilty with a two year jail sentence."

Donovan didn't hesitate, "Are you kidding me? No way in hell!"

Mr. Johnson laughed. "I really didn't think you would go for it but I'm required by law to ask."

Donovan hangs up the phone mumbling to himself, "Do I look that stupid?"

"What's wrong?" I asked.

He told me what Michael's lawyer was trying to do. "They must be crazy! The only reason he would think we would go for that is either he is crazy, which we both know he is, or he thinks we are ready to be done with this."

186

I hugged him. "Don't let it get you down."

Back in court the Judge brought everybody to order and announced that there would be no more continuances or delays and we would be there all day every day until the case went to the jury because she was ready to have the cameras out of her courtroom.

The defense started with trying to deny any of it ever happened. The prosecution countered with all of the overwhelming evidence so it's obvious that strategy isn't going to work. The defense then tried to make it look like everything that happened, even the attack, was my fault. I could see the hatred in Donovan's eyes for Michael. "I should have killed him when I had the chance," he mumbled.

Just when I thought I had seen it all, the defense started entering things into evidence that point the finger at me and not Michael. Donovan had given me the money to pay off Michael so it looked like I had paid Michael to hire someone to kill Donovan. Donovan looked at me and said, "I know what he is trying to do and so help me he won't get away with it."

Even though I had nothing to do with any of this they were making it look like I did. I felt horrible. How could anyone ever do this to someone else? When court ended for the day Mr. Johnson told us he wanted to speak with us and asked us to come to his office. At his office he starts, "Donovan, they have another plea I need to discuss with you. They only have to create reasonable doubt for the attempted murder charge. They don't have a leg to stand on with the assault charge because of the videos and witnesses that were there. So he will be doing time for that regardless. The plea they offered is he will plead guilty and serve five years on top of whatever the judge gives him for the assault charge."

Donovan turned to me. "They are trying to pin this all on you. If I take the deal they will leave you alone."

I shook my head. "Donovan, don't you even think about it. I can take care of myself and there is no way I'm going to let him get out of this. Don't take the deal because of me. I say fight."

Donovan asked Mr. Johnson, "How does it look for him?"

Mr. Johnson shook his head. "Well, I would say it looks good for him, but tomorrow we are going to enter the assault into evidence and once the jury puts the two incidents together they will see a pattern hopefully."

"And if they don't?"

"Well, if they don't then he could get an acquittal."

Donovan thought long and hard before he asked, "Can we give it one more day?"

Mr. Johnson shrugged his shoulders. "I don't see why not. We will see how tomorrow goes and talk about it when we recess for lunch."

The party I was catering that night went well. Once again nobody mentioned the accident. It's like everybody in this town has nothing but respect for Donovan and doesn't want to add to the heartbreak he is already dealing with. He couldn't talk about anything other than Constance and me. I walked up in the middle of one of his conversations to overhear him pushing the catering business. I smiled and walked off. I don't want him to know that I know he is helping me.

Court came early after a long night. Hopefully today would be the last day of testimony and then we can just wait on a verdict. It really would be nice to put all of this behind us before we move. Then once we get moved it will be like a fresh start for all of us without all of the drama.

The judge brought the court to order and testimony began. The defense put Michael on the stand and he lied under oath but I wouldn't expect anything less from him. The prosecution attorney knew he was lying and tore him apart on the stand. "So Michael, isn't it true that you assaulted Mr. Donovan at an earlier time?"

Michael tried to explain that, "Yes, I did but only because –"

The attorney cut him off, "And isn't it true, Michael, that Mr. Donovan took everything away from you? Your girlfriend, your career, and hundreds of thousands of dollars?"

Michael tried to look suave. "Yes, but –"

Again the attorney cut him off, "Didn't you pay someone to stab Mr. Donovan at an after-party?"

Michael tried to deny it but the attorney told the Judge he had nothing further. During the questioning I watched the jury and honestly I couldn't tell which way they were leaning.

The guy that stabbed Donovan was called to take the stand and as he did Donovan's grip on my hand tightened. He gave the same story he gave to the police about Michael hiring him and paying him thousands of dollars. He sounded very convincing to me but it's hard for me to be objective because I know the truth. If I were on the jury I don't know how I would vote.

We meet Mr. Johnson for lunch to discuss the plea deal. "Donovan, it looks to me like the jury is buying it. I can't say for certain but I wouldn't go with the plea if I were you," Mr. Johnson informed him.

Donovan looked to me for what he should do. "I don't know what I would do honestly but if you only take the plea because of me then I will say it again, don't."

Donovan thanked Mr. Johnson and said he would

take his chances.

We went back for closing arguments and the case went to the jury. We leave the courthouse and went to sign the papers on our new house.

If everything goes according to plan we will be getting the keys so we can move in over the weekend. I just wanted everything settled so we could slow down. As we were leaving the realty office I told Donovan, "You know, since we have so much going on I turned the parties I had planned over to Steph for the weekend so we could get moved. It's really the only time we will have to do it. It's going to be a long couple of days but I think we can do it."

Donovan grinned at me. "Oh babe, you amuse me sometimes. There is no way we can get all that done in a weekend, but I already took care of it. I have to come clean. When I took you to look at the house I had already seen it and put a down payment on it. I knew you would love it and if you didn't for some reason I could have gotten my money back so it wasn't a hard decision."

I smiled at him. "You seem to have it all figured out, don't you? I love the way you know me, but what do you mean you already took care of it?"

He leaned over and kissed me on the nose. "I have movers due to be at your house and mine Friday evening. Everything will be moved for us. All we have to do is unpack and decorate, which I thought we would do together."

If he only knew how much I loved him. He always manages to take care of me even when he should be taking care of himself. He has had so much going on I haven't bothered to tell him I haven't been feeling myself since the accident. I chalked it up to stress figuring I would be fine as soon as some of this was off our plates.

190

I had a party tonight but Donovan said he would rather stay with the kids, which isn't completely out of the ordinary. We had been talking about Constance getting all of the attention and he knew the boys would love some of his time. He sent Steph and me to do the party. It was a long night and I couldn't wait to get back home.

I crawled into bed next to Donovan and he rolled over and put his arms around me. "I feel so safe in your arms," I said dreamily which brought an amazing smile to his face.

"Well, I hope you're still happy when I tell you what I'm about to tell you."

I felt my stomach tie in knots. "What happened?"

"Nothing happened, and I know you're exhausted but we have a date Saturday night. Since you took the weekend off I thought that would be the best time to do it."

I looked at him puzzled. "Do what? Just because we don't have work doesn't mean we have nothing to do."

"I know babe, but we are going on a date. Just you and I and it's a surprise so don't start asking a bunch of questions," he said chuckling and leaving no room for argument.

At my house we settled in for a family night. We ate dinner and watched a movie. Once all the kids were in bed Donovan and I went for a walk on the beach. The full moon was just over the horizon and its reflection danced on the water. We sat together in the sand and looked out over the ocean.

"It's so beautiful out here," I said.

"Not as beautiful as you," Donovan whispered. He pointed toward the moon and asked, "Can you see that small island over there?"

I squinted. "Yeah, barely," I admitted. I could see the silhouette of the trees in the moon.

"That is my special place here in California. Whenever I'm having trouble I borrow my friend's boat and go over there. There is never anyone over there so it's quiet and peaceful. I will have to take you over there sometime."

"I would really like that," I said. I kissed him fervently and we made love in the sand.

CHAPTER 16

Donovan took the kids and Steph out the next day. My stomach was in knots thinking about how much we had to do this weekend. We still hadn't received a verdict yet but we were moving and even with movers there was so much to be done. Somehow we had to unpack and still make time for our date that Donovan had planned for us. Luckily he was flying in his and Jonathan's parents to help. I didn't know what I would do without him. He had become my rock and the kids absolutely adored him.

The house was so quiet with everyone out for the day. In the short time we have been here we have made so many memories. I was actually going to miss this place. I spent the day packing and finally had things ready for the movers. Donovan called to tell me he was picking up the parents at the airport and that he would stop and get dinner so I had nothing left to do.

I sat on the couch thinking back over my life and how I got to this point. I never thought losing someone I loved so much could ever get better but here I am with someone that I love as much as I loved Jonathan. My thoughts were interrupted when everyone got home.

We sat at the table, one big happy family, for the last time and enjoyed our meal. Afterwards the kids were in their rooms throwing their toys into boxes when Donovan's phone rang. He answered, listened for a second, and then said, "We are on our way."

After he hung up the phone he announced to us, "They have a verdict. We'll be back."

We rode to the courthouse in silence; both scared that the verdict might not go our way. When everyone arrived the bailiff called court to order. The judge came in and announced that they would do sentencing directly after reading the verdict. The jurors were brought in and seated. The bailiff approached the foreperson, took the verdict, and handed it to the Judge.

He gave it back to the foreperson and the Judge asked, "Madam Foreperson, is this your verdict?"

She rose. "Yes, your honor."

"Please read it to the court."

She opened it and read, "In the matter of the State of California versus Michael Stargate on count one of assault, we the jury find the defendant guilty."

Donovan squeezed my hand and I heard him stop breathing.

"In the matter of the State of California versus Michael Stargate on count two of attempted murder, we the jury find the defendant guilty."

The courtroom erupted in cheers. Donovan hugged and kissed me. The Judge called the court back to order. "Are you ready to impose sentencing madam foreperson?"

"We are your honor. On count one, assault; we sentence the defendant to six months in prison."

Donovan looked at me and whispered, "They are going easy on him. I can't believe he is going to get away with this."

The foreperson continued, "On count two, attempted murder, we sentence the defendant to forty years, eligible for parole in twenty years."

We watched as they handcuffed Michael. They were leading him out when he turned and hollered at Donovan, "This isn't over."

It is over enough for us for right now though. We left the courthouse feeling as justice had been served.

When we got back to the house they were putting the last of the stuff in the moving truck. Donovan asked the guy if they had any word on his house. He was told that it had been packed and was on its way. It looks like we will be unpacking tonight.

I climbed out of bed and looked out the window at the water shimmering as the first rays of sunlight hit it. It was breathtaking. Donovan wrapped his arms around me. "It's almost as beautiful as you. I think it's a sign that we are going to have a beautiful life together." I sure hoped he was right. I still had butterflies from all of the big changes coming up.

Donovan told me he had set up a girl's day out and the guys would take care of the unpacking. We left and went shopping, did lunch, and visited the salon. All in all it was a great day but there was one more surprise in store.

Mrs. Sara told me, "We are going back to the house, but you have an appointment with a masseur to help you relax a little. We will see you later." She kissed me on the cheek and smiled at me before they left. The massage was just what I needed. I was so relaxed and invigorated, which was just perfect for my date tonight.

I walked in the house a couple hours later and there were people everywhere unpacking but I don't know any of them. Someone walked up and addressed me, "Ms. Sherri?" I nodded my head. "This is for you. Have a good night," he said and handed me a note. The note was from Donovan and read:

Sherri, my love, I am going to give you what I hope will be a night you will never forget. Get dressed and you will know what to do after that.

I will know what to do after that? I didn't have a clue what I was supposed to do after that but I went to get

195

dressed. It took me forever. I couldn't decide what to wear and Donovan didn't tell me where we were going so I could dress accordingly. I decided on a beautiful summer dress that I thought would fit in wherever we were going.

I opened the door hoping for another clue, which I found. Rose petals scattered in a path on the floor. I followed them through the house, out the back door, and there on a boat was Donovan, waiting.

"Come on, babe. I'm taking you to my special place," he said.

I got on the boat and my heart skipped a beat as I took a minute to admire how devastatingly handsome he was.

"You always do too much for me. I didn't need all of this," I told him, though it was an amazing start to what promised to be a phenomenal date.

He smiled at me. "I know, babe, but tonight is a special night. Everything is starting to fall into place for us and I wanted to celebrate." I definitely couldn't argue with that.

We took the boat to the island he showed me the night before. There on the beach was a cabana set up with a candlelit dinner for two. "Donovan, it's perfect. Thank you so much. I couldn't ask for more."

We sat to eat but unfortunately I didn't have much of an appetite. I had something on my mind that I needed to talk to him about but I didn't want to ruin the night. He noticed I wasn't eating and asked, "Is everything okay, babe?"

I started to tell him but decided against it. "Yeah. I'm fine. Just not really hungry."

He held his hand out. "May I have this dance?"

I smiled at him. "But, Donovan, there is no music."

Almost on cue the music started to play. I took his hand and we danced. It was truly a magical night.

"Donovan, the only thing that would make this night any better is if our family and friends could celebrate with us," I whispered to him as we twirled to the music.

We stopped dancing and he smiled at me. "This way, babe." He turned us around and said, "Lights, please." A path magically appeared through the trees. We walked down the path to a clearing where there were lights hanging from the trees and all our friends and family had gathered.

"Surprise!!" they exclaimed.

I was so stunned that I fainted. When I came to I saw that Donovan was holding me, Mrs. Sara was wiping my head with a rag and cold water, and Mrs. Rosa was fanning me.

"What happened?" I asked.

Donovan leaned over and kissed me on the nose. "I guess you were too overwhelmed and you fainted."

I started to get up. "I'm so sorry y'all. I don't know what happened."

Donovan helped me up and wouldn't stop fussing over me. "I'm fine. I'll be okay. Thank you for doing this. I know I have been distracted tonight but you doing this tells me I'm doing the right thing."

Donovan looked at me puzzled. "What are you talking about?"

I put my hand on his cheek and said, "Give me a minute and you will understand."

I regained my composure and said, "Constance, come here sweetie." She came over to me and I asked, "Are you ready?"

She smiled and said, "Yeah, mom. Let's do it."

Donovan looked at me in total confusion.

"Can I have everyone's attention please? I'm so glad you're all here. There has been so much going on and I wanted to take this opportunity to say thank you for all your love and support through this all, especially you

Donovan. My family and I couldn't ask for better family and friends." I looked at Constance and in a low voice admitted, "I didn't know I would be so nervous doing this." I looked back at everyone else and continued, "I was waiting for the right time, and with all of you being here I can't think of a better time to announce that Constance and I have discussed it and have decided, if he will do it, we would like to make Donovan Constance's new manager."

He looked at me as the tears pooled in his eyes. "Sherri, are you sure?"

I kissed him on the nose and said, "I'm absolutely sure and so is Constance."

He looked at her for confirmation and she smiled and nodded her head yes. He picked her up. "Well, if you're both sure."

I hugged them both. "We are so sure that all you have to do is say yes and sign the papers. I talked to Mr. Johnson about this shortly after we heard that you couldn't return to singing immediately and had him draw up the papers and I already signed them."

He said, "Well what can I say then, but yes!"

Everybody cheered and began congratulating us. A minute later he asked, "Wait, what are you trying to do here?"

I looked at him mystified. "I thought you would be happy."

He grinned. "Well, this was my night. Are you trying to upstage me here?"

Huh? What is he talking about? I was so confused. "What..."

He stepped back and everybody got extremely quiet. His dad handed him something and he got down on one knee, opened the box and asked, "Sherri, Constance, Charlie, and Drew, will you marry me and be my family?"

I gasped and fainted again. When I came around the

second time Donovan was talking to me, "I'm so sorry, Sherri. I know it's too soon. I wanted to wait, but I just couldn't."

I looked at him and smiled. "No, it's okay. Let's try it again. I promise to stay standing this time."

He laughed. "Well, I think maybe you should stay sitting." He took the ring out of the box and asked again, "Will you marry me?"

I said yes and hugged him. "There is only one problem," I told him. He looked at me and I kissed him. "I'm not trying to be picky here, but there is more than just me, Constance, Charlie, and Drew that you have to consider."

He laughed again. "Well, I thought if I included Steph in there it might be weird."

I turned and looked at all the loving people that were here with us tonight then back at him, "No, that's not what I mean. I'm not trying to upstage you here but there is a plus one to that list."

He looks at me even more perplexed. "What are you trying to tell me?"

I took his hand and placed it on my stomach. "Donovan, I'm pregnant."

His mouth hit the ground. "Are you sure?" he asked timidly.

I laughed. "Well, I haven't been feeling myself and I thought it was just stress but while I was getting dressed I took a test and it was positive."

He had the biggest smile on his face as he turned and hollered, "I'm going to be a daddy, again!"

I look at him questioningly, "Again?"

He took Constance, Charlie, and Drew in his arms. "Yes again. I already have three kids."

He let them go, picked me up, and kissed me with so much love and passion that it made my knees weak and took my breath away.

Life couldn't be better. I started this adventure as a half that I thought would never be whole again but it's amazing what life can throw at you.

Preview of
Writing On The Wall

Writing on the Wall
Chapter 1

It had been a month since my life changed so much on that little island off the coast of California. Things were finally starting to settle down. Donovan and I had decided to wait until after the baby to plan the wedding. Constance's career seemed to be moving rapidly in the right direction. Charlie and Drew seemed to be adjusting quite well and were excited about starting their new school. Best of all, there had been no word from Michael since his sentencing.

"Good morning beautiful," Donovan said kissing me on the cheek. "We need to get moving, unfortunately."

I wrinkled my nose at him. "Do we really have to?"

He wrapped me up in his arms. "Well, I guess five more minutes won't hurt anyone."

We snuggled down in the bed with every intention of making the most of the five minutes we had given ourselves when the kids come busting through the door all of them talking at once.

Donovan sat up in the bed laughing, "Well I guess that wasn't going to last."

I started to apologize. "Donovan, I'm so sor-"

He put his finger over my mouth. "Don't you dare start apologizing."

He grabbed all three kids and wrapped them in a bear hug. From the middle I heard Drew, "Donovan, I love you but your squishing me."

He let them all go and they settled on the bed in front of us. They were each looking at the other with these "you do it" looks on their faces. Finally Drew turned to Donovan and said, "Donovan, they are scared to ask but I'm not." He paused, looking at them and then back at

Donovan. He crawled over and settled in Donovan's lap and turned again to Constance and Charlie who were pushing him to finish. He gave them an irritated look and turned his attention back to Donovan. He took Donovan's face in his little hands and said, "Now Donovan, this is a very serious talk we need to have and I need you to focus because your answer is very important."

Donovan put his nose to Drew's. "You have my undivided attention."

Drew took his hands down from Donovan's face, took a deep breath, and began, "Now, you have to hear everything before you make a decision," he said, acting all grown up. "Constance, Charlie, and me have been talking and we wanted to ask you…" His voice trailed off.

"Drew, are you okay? You know you can ask me anything," Donovan assured him patting his head.

Drew looked at me and back at Donovan with Constance and Charlie poking him trying to hurry him along.

"OKAY! I'm doing it! Stop!" he yelled at them and turned back to Donovan. "We were wondering if you would be upset if we called you something besides Donovan."

My jaw hit the floor because I knew what was coming next. Donovan, oblivious to the whole ordeal, looked at Drew puzzled. "Well, what else would you call me?"

Drew threw his arms in the air exasperated. "Well, duh! We would call you daddy."

It was Donovan's turn to pick his jaw up off the floor. All three kids looked at him intensely waiting on an answer. He turned to me and I just gave him a "you're on your own" look.

He turned back to them and took each of their hands in his and attempted to explain. "Y'all know I'm not your dad-"

Before he could say anything else Drew interrupted. "We know you're not our real dad and we don't want you to replace him but you're the next best thing. Would it help if we called you daddy two?"

I found myself utterly amazed at the intelligence of my five-year-old. Donovan erupted in laughter. "Well I guess that answers all of my questions."

The three of them sat waiting on an answer and were starting to get upset. I shoved him playfully, "Are you going to give them an answer or just make them suffer?"

He leaned over and kissed each of them on the forehead before saying, "I would be honored if you called me daddy."

I looked at him laughing. "So daddy, what do you think we should do first today?"

Before he could answer all three kids started to chant, "EAT! EAT! EAT!"

We went downstairs and the kids ran to the table arguing the whole way about who got to sit next to "daddy". Donovan put his arms around me. "It's such a shame they don't love me," he said, chuckling.

Before we could sit down the phone rang. I knew it was Stephanie calling for her daily check in. I had sent her to spend a couple of weeks with Steve, her boyfriend, while he was in from offshore.

"Hello?" I answered.

"Hey! How are things? Do you need me home yet?" Steph asked without breathing.

I started laughing. "No, I think daddy and I have it for now."

A loud cheer erupted from behind me at the mention of daddy.

"We are going to need you here this weekend though for Constance's birthday party."

The line went silent. Finally, I added, "If you're not ready-"

Before I could finish she interrupted, "No, that's fine. I'm actually coming in this afternoon."

There was a brief pause and she added, "There is something we need to talk about and it's kind of important."

Of course, I couldn't let her say something like that and leave me hanging. "Steph, what's going on? Is everything okay?"

Steph stopped me before I could start my interrogation, "Everything will be fine. We just need to talk. I'm coming in at one thirty. Are one of you going to pick me up or do I need to take a cab?"

The feeling in the pit of my stomach told me this couldn't be good. "I'll be there to get you."

She said nothing more than "okay" and hung up.

I replaced the phone in the cradle and turned to Donovan completely distraught. He, of course, kept a level head, wrapped his arms around me, and asked, "What happened?"

"I...I...I," I stammered, "I don't know. She just said we needed to talk and it was important."

He smiled slightly. "Sherri you are freaking out over something you don't even know about again. It could be something good. You need to stop worrying so much about things you can't control." He gently kisses me on the forehead and dried my eyes.

I caught my breath and sat down, "You're right. I have to stop letting myself get all worked up. It's not good for me or the baby."

He leaned down, put his hand on my stomach, and chuckled, "Yeah, our little Jackson isn't going to be happy if mama keeps getting him all upset."

He knew how to make me smile. "Him, huh? Who said it was going to be a him?"

Constance interrupted, "It just can't be another boy! MOM! We are already outnumbered here. You have to make it a girl!"

Donovan patted her on the head. "Don't worry, sweet pea. If this one is a boy I guess mommy and I will just have to try again for a girl. Right, mom?"

I started laughing. "I think we will have to discuss that another time. We haven't even gotten this one here yet so let's not go volunteering mom for another one just yet."

Donovan agreed to take the kids for the day so that I could pick up Steph and we could talk privately. Between the anticipation and the morning sickness, my breakfast was determined not to stay down.

I arrived at the airport an hour early because I was so ready to find out exactly what was going on. I had plenty of time to kill so I went to the coffee shop to have a glass of water and a bagel to maybe calm my stomach. I grabbed a magazine and found a seat.

I was thumbing through the magazine when I ran across an article on Michael and I couldn't help but read it. The more I read the angrier I got. I was so absorbed I must have lost track of time because Steph put her hand on my shoulder and scared me half to death.

"Sherri, are you ready?"

I looked up at her visibly shaken. "Yeah, let's get out of here."

She sat down across the table. "What's going on? What are you reading?"

She took the magazine and looked at the article. With her mouth on the floor she asked, "Are they serious? How can he do this?"

I snatched the magazine from her and shoved it in my purse. "Let's not even think about that right now. I will call Mr. Johnson when we get home and deal with it then."

I stood up but she didn't move. Looking at the floor she quietly said, "That's what I wanted to talk to you about."

My knees started to go weak so I sat back down. "You already knew about this? Why haven't you said something before now?"

She could hear the anger in my voice as she looked up at me. "No Sherri, I knew nothing about this I promise. I meant we needed to talk about going home."

I look at her puzzled and irritated. "Steph, just spit it out. After this, I honestly don't have the patience to try to drag it out of you."

She hesitated and slowly started, "Well, it may be a good thing. I'm not really sure but I didn't want to say anything over the phone in case it upset you."

I threw my hands in the air. "Steph, are you going to tell me or am I going to have to wait to hear it on the news?"

She could see my patience was really wearing thin. "I'm sorry. You know I hate upsetting people and I'm just worried this is going to upset you is all." She took a deep breath and continued, "Well, it seems that Steve has lost his job. He wants to move out here to be with me."

I calmed myself. "Well Steph, you know he is practically one of the family and I'm not going to leave him out in the cold."

She looked at the table and started fidgeting. "That's not it, Sherri. He and I will get our own place.

That's part of it. I know you're going to need help with the kids and I didn't want to just move out on you."

I let out a sigh of relief. "Steph, you know I will always need you but I understand you have to live your life. I don't expect you to live your life for us forever. I think I have the perfect solution for all of us."

She looked at me relieved. "I'm so glad you understand and I want to hear your solution but there is one more thing I need to tell you and I really hope you take it as well as you just took this."

I could feel my stomach starting to churn again and I thought to myself, *calm down Sherri, jeez. You can't keep getting all worked up over stuff.*

Steph continued, "The only real problem with the whole thing I guess is Nick."

I looked at her puzzled. Nick is Steve's best friend but they couldn't be more different. Nick was a typical roughneck but under his tough exterior was a heart of gold as long as he was sober. He had shoulder length dirty blonde hair, blue eyes that sparkled like water when the sun hit it, and he was well built to say the least but that came from years of manual labor. Nick and I had a thing not long after Jonathan died until he got drunk one night and thought he was going to manhandle me. I defended myself and apparently a girl getting the better of him was more than he could handle. The last I heard he had gotten really bad on drugs.

"Steph, just so we are clear, Nick will not be living in my house."

She quickly stopped me, "Oh no. I would never put you in the position of asking you that but I wanted to let you know that after Steve and I get a place he is planning on moving out here with us. Sherri, he has really changed and cleaned himself up. He isn't on drugs anymore and he's stopped drinking. He wanted me to give you a message but I told him he was on his own as far as you were concerned because I wasn't going to have you mad at me because of him."

"Honestly, Steph, when he crossed the line and put his hands on me I was done with him. I know he is Steve's friend and all, but he is dead to me and nothing he can say or do will change that."

She looked at me knowingly. "I figured that much which is why I told him to leave me out of it. I thought I should let you know what his plans were so he didn't just pop up on you one day."

I stood up again. "Well, I'm glad you did. We should get back to the house so we can deal with this Michael situation and the kids are dying to see you. I swear even behind bars he is doing his best to make sure I'm miserable."

She stood up as well. "Would you expect anything less from him?"

Guess she has a point.

Once in the car I started to tell her about the weekend coming up. "It's going to be really hectic this weekend and I'm going to really need your help. BTR has volunteered to play for the party and Constance is ecstatic about it. Donovan has hired a maid, at least until after the baby is born, and we have decorators coming Saturday morning. You will have to do most of the cooking since I have to decorate the cake." I let out a big sigh, "And I will need you to pick up everyone at the airport."

Steph looked at me. "Why did you say it like that? Who is everyone?"

I looked at her disgusted. "You wouldn't believe me if I told you."

She chuckled. "Try me."

"Well, of course, Mrs. Sara and Mr. Donnie, and Donovan is flying Steve in for you. Then there's Mrs. Rosa and Mr. Jacob," I hesitated.

She laughed, "I can believe it. I wouldn't expect them not to be here."

I put my hand up stopping her, "No, here is the one you're not going to believe...Theresa."

Her mouth was on the ground, "Your mother?"

I just laughed. "I know, right? Donovan has been on me lately about patching up our relationship and he thinks bringing her out here will do that."

Steph laughed heartily. "Yeah, lets rub the fact that you were right and she was wrong in her face. That will make things all better."

Both of us laughed and I said, "I know, but he keeps reminding me that family is the most important thing and I should give her a chance so I just got tired of arguing about it and gave in."

She reached over and felt my forehead for fever. "Are you feeling okay? It's not like you to just give in."

I pushed her hand back playfully. "I'm fine, but he isn't going to understand until he sees it with his own eyes. Trust me, one smart ass remark and he will see a side of me he doesn't want to."

Steph chuckled. "With her, smart ass remarks are practically a given."

We pulled up at the house and three very excited kids were waiting in the yard. They all came running and screaming all different things at once. Steph bent down and gave them all hugs and said, "I can't understand everyone talking at once so let's try one at a time. Constance you go first since you're oldest."

Constance started jumping up and down, "BTR is going to play at my party this weekend." She stopped and looked at Stephanie with a grown up look. "That's Big Time Rush but all us kids call them BTR."

Steph started laughing. "Yeah, I know who they are." She turned to Charlie, "And what's going on with you?"

He gave her a hug. "Nothing really. I just really missed you and am glad your home."

Drew was bouncing around. "Is it my turn? Is it? Is it?"

Steph laughed, "Yes, Drew, it's your turn. What's going on in your world?"

Drew stopped bouncing and motioned for her to come closer. "We all decided that we are going to call Donovan daddy." She tried to look surprised but she already knew.

We finally got everybody inside and settled after our reunion in the yard. The kids had calmed down enough to go upstairs and play, which left us adults to talk. We sat down and I pulled the magazine out of my purse and quietly placed it on the table.

Donovan gave me a questioning glance. "What's that?"

I tried to figure out how to tell him about the article without upsetting him. Since the accident the mere mention of Michael's name sent him into a state of mind I didn't like. "Donovan," I started slowly, "I need you to stay calm and not get agitated with what I'm about to tell you."

He looked at me. "If it involves Michael I can't make any promises but I will try."

I looked at Steph worried and then back at Donovan. "According to this article, Michael is trying to get his sentence overturned on a technicality. His lawyer, Mr. Jackson, is trying to say there is new evidence and that the jury was tainted. They want his attempted murder conviction reversed and him to be released on time served for the assault charge."

He sat there quietly trying to absorb the whole thing. I was starting to think maybe he had calmed down with the whole situation when he slammed his hands down on the table and jumped up.

As he headed for the door I heard him mumbling to himself. "I swear I should have killed him when I had the chance. Sorry son of a –" His voice trailed off as he grabbed his jacket.

I jumped up and ran towards him hollering, "Donovan! Where are you –"

Before I could finish the door slammed behind him. I turned to Steph and she was standing there like a deer caught in the headlights. The phone rang startling us back to reality.

I ran over and picked it up, "Donovan, what the…"

Mr. Johnson interrupted, "Sherri, it's Mr. Johnson. I was actually calling for Donovan but I'm assuming he isn't there if you thought I was him."

My heart sank. "No Mr. Johnson, he just left. He is very upset over this Michael situation."

Mr. Johnson replied, "Well, honestly I don't think they have a leg to stand on but I haven't seen the briefs on the case yet either. Y'all shouldn't worry and I will call back as soon as I have news."

I hung up the phone and wobbled back to sit down. Steph and I sat there, neither of us knowing what to say. Finally Steph broke the ice, "I'm sure he will be fine. He can't get to Michael to kill him. He will calm down and be back. Why don't you tell me about this solution you were talking about at the airport?"

She was trying to distract me but it wasn't going to work. I may talk about other things but my mind wasn't going to stop worrying about Donovan. "I will have to talk to Donovan about it of course but I was thinking we could fire the maid and just pay you to help me with the house and the kids. What we are paying her should help you and Steve until he can get a job. Y'all could start looking for a place this weekend and as long as it's reasonable I will help y'all get it as a housewarming present."

She looked at me. "Sherri, not that I don't appreciate that, but are you forgetting what's going to happen when we get our own place? I will take the job but I would think you would want to prolong Nick coming as long as possible."

I just laughed. "Steph, like I said before he is dead to me so I am not worried about him coming. He isn't going to make a difference in my life one way or the other."

She walked over and hugged me. "Then yes, that would be wonderful. I just don't want to cause you any more stress than you're already dealing with. Lets work on the party menu or something. We have a ton to do and you need a distraction." She put her hand on my shoulder. "He will be okay, Sherri, and he will be back."

I jumped up. "Why am I sitting here stressing? I'll just call him. Duh!" I said, smiling.

I grabbed the phone and as I dialed the last digit it started to ring. With every ring my heart beat faster and faster worried that he wouldn't answer. Finally someone answered. "Hello?"

Okay, definitely not Donovan's voice. Who the hell is answering his phone? I wondered to myself.

I hesitated before asking, "Could I speak to Donovan please?"

The guy on the other end was rude in a polite way when he said, "He can't get to the phone right now but I will tell him you called," then abruptly hung up.

I stood there staring at the phone trying to figure out what had just happened. Steph walked over and asked, "What was that all about?"

I slowly put the phone on the table with my mouth wide open.

"Sherri!" Steph shouted snapping her fingers in my face. "Who was that?"

I snapped back to reality. "Honestly Steph, I have no idea but he was kind of rude. I don't know why but I get the feeling Donovan is okay. How does that happen?"

She just stared at me not sure what to say. "Do you feel like working on the menu for the party? Maybe if we can get that done I can take the kids with me and go to the store so you can relax. You have had a hell of a day."

She brought me a pen and paper and sat down next to me. "What should we do? Are we going full-blown dinner party or just little kid's party?" she asked laughing.

"Well," I began, "I think we aren't going full-blown dinner party but a little more than just a kid's party." I managed a smile as I continued, "This is after all Hollywood."

We sat there silently with blank expressions on our faces. I still couldn't think straight. After a few minutes I finally started, "Well, we will have cake and ice cream, of course, punch to drink, and I think maybe just some finger foods for the adults. What do you think?"

Steph laughed. "You're asking me? I don't even know who is coming or how many kids will be here or anything. You're asking the wrong person."

I tried to get my brain to function but there was only one thing on it at the moment. If only Donovan would come home or call then everything would be fine. I don't want to be unappreciative at the fact that Steph was trying to distract me but it's just so hard to focus right now.

I got up to get a glass of water from the kitchen and turned back to Steph, "Everybody that was here for our last party will be here and they are all bringing kids."

Steph started chuckling. "What are they going to do, kidnap some?"

I couldn't help but laugh at that. "No, actually they are bringing nieces, nephews, and some kids from the orphanage. Several of them are big brothers and big sisters to kids who have no family. They asked if it would be okay and, of course, I'm not going to say no. I think it will be good for Constance to be around kids that don't have as much as she does. I really don't want fame going to her head."

Steph looked amazed. "That's just awesome, Sherri. Those kids will really enjoy that and it will set a good example for Constance. In this town she is going to need all the help she can get keeping her image clean." She thought for a minute before continuing, "Well, I would suggest keeping it simple for the adults."

I grinned. "You're just saying that because you're the one having to cook it all."

We laughed and sat back at the table to get started. I grabbed a pen and immediately started writing as fast as I could.

"Whoa there, woman," Steph said jokingly. "What are you volunteering me to cook while you're writing so fast?"

I chuckled. "You'll be just fine. We are going to do mini pigs-in-a-blanket, party-shaped sandwiches, and then some chips and a couple of homemade dips. I need you to grab the stuff for the goody bags as well, mostly candy and toys, but I was also thinking gift certificates of some sort. Any ideas?"

I saw a light bulb go off over Steph's head, so to speak. "Why not do it for music then they can get Constance's CD if they want."

I snickered. "That's actually a great idea. Okay, so here is the list," I said as I passed the paper to her. "Do you think you can handle it and the kids?"

She put her hand up. "I know you did not just ask me that."

We both giggled at the thought. She rounded up the kids and headed out the door.

With the house finally to myself all I wanted and needed to do was to try to relax but I just couldn't see that happening until I knew what was going on with Donovan. I settled on to the couch to try to watch some TV and maybe enjoy the peace and quiet while everyone was gone when the doorbell rang.

I opened the door to a rather attractive guy standing about five foot nine with shaggy brown hair, bright brown eyes, and what appeared to be a very nice body. I stared and zoned out apparently, as I usually do, because I didn't hear anything he said.

He reached out and touched my shoulder. "Hello? Are you okay?"

I feigned a smile. "Yes, I'm sorry. Just a lot going on today. Can I help you?"

He flashed the most gorgeous smile I had seen in quite a while, next to Donovan's, of course. "Are you Sherri?"

I was honestly scared to answer that question with the way things had been going. Nonetheless I said, "Yes, I'm Sherri. Is there something I can do for you?"

He kind of chuckled and said, "No, but I think I have something that belongs to you." With that he turned and walked away.

Huh? Talk about odd. If he has something that belongs to me why did he leave?

I walked out to see what he was doing and saw him helping someone out of the car. I gasped when I realized it was Donovan. As I ran over I noticed he was hardly walking on his own and only semi-conscious.

© *June 2011*

www.ingramcontent.com/pod-product-compliance
Lightning Source LLC
Chambersburg PA
CBHW031309120626
46554CB00001BA/349